PENGUIN BOOKS

IT'S A BATTLEFIELD

Graham Greene was born in 1904 and educated at Berkhamsted School, where his father was the headmaster. On coming down from Balliol College, Oxford, where he published a book of verse, he worked for three years as a sub-editor on *The Times*. He established his reputation with his fourth novel, *Stamboul Train*. In 1935 he made a journey across Liberia, described in *Journey Without Maps*, and on his return was appointed film critic of the *Spectator*. In 1926 he had been received into the Roman Catholic Church and was commissioned to visit Mexico in 1938, and report on the religious persecution there. As a result he wrote *The Lawless Roads* and, later, *The Power and the Glory*.

Brighton Rock* was published in 1938, and in 1940 he became literary editor of the *Spectator*. The next year he undertook work for the Foreign Office and was sent out to Sierra Leone in 1941–3. One of his major post-war novels, *The Heart of the Matter*, is set in West Africa and is considered by many to be his finest book. This was followed by *The End of the Affair*, *The Quiet American*, a story set in Vietnam, *Our Man in Havana*, and *A Burnt-Out Case*. *The Comedians* and twelve other novels have been filmed, plus two of his short stories, and *The Third Man* was first written as a film treatment. In 1967 he published a collection of short stories under the title *May We Borrow Your Husband?*

In all, Graham Greene has written some thirty novels, edited 'entertainments', plays, children's books, travel books, and collections of essays and short stories. Among his latest publications are his long-awaited autobiography, *A Sort of Life* (1971), *The Pleasure Dome* (1972), *The Honorary Consul* (1973), *Lord Rochester's Monkey* (1974), *An Impossible Woman: the Memories of Dottoressa Moor of Capri* (edited; 1975) and *The Human Factor* (1978). He was made a Companion of Honour in 1966.

GRAHAM GREENE

IT'S A BATTLEFIELD (London)

Beginning of his major achievement

PENGUIN BOOKS

Penguin Books Ltd, Harmondsworth, Middlesex, England
Penguin Books, 625 Madison Avenue, New York, New York 10022, U.S.A.
Penguin Books Australia Ltd, Ringwood, Victoria, Australia
Penguin Books Canada Ltd, 2801 John Street, Markham, Ontario, Canada L3R 1B4
Penguin Books (N.Z.) Ltd, 182–190 Wairau Road, Auckland 10, New Zealand

—

First published in Great Britain by William Heinemann 1934
Published in Penguin Books in Great Britain 1940
Reprinted 1971, 1976, 1977

First published in the United States of America by Doubleday 1934
Published in the United States of America by The Viking Press 1962
Published in Penguin Books in the United States of America 1977

—

Printed in the United States of America by
Offset Paperback Mfrs., Inc., Dallas, Pennsylvania
Set in Intertype Times

Prison Triads

Press factory

Drovers - triad - Milly, Jim, Conrad

Ass't commissions + housekeeper

'In so far as the battlefield presented itself to the bare eyesight of men, it had no entirety, no length, no breadth, no depth, no size, no shape, and was made up of nothing except small numberless circlets commensurate with such ranges of vision as the mist might allow at each spot. . . . In such conditions, each separate gathering of English soldiery went on fighting its own little battle in happy and advantageous ignorance of the general state of the action; nay, even very often in ignorance of the fact that any great conflict was raging.'

Episodes - Circularity, beyond particles, Kinglake

Jaste - positions, relationships, arrangement, in context art of

Language, symbol, coding

Reflects back increasing meaning, layer

Scope in looking at world in cross purposes

Capability of evil in his Catholicity

(Disaster is always around the corner)

Jamesian + Greene version of universe

Texture - Need, to penetrate society

Pace - fade out, juxta - position for film

Left Caroline - Ass't commissioner - beyond little battles (agape Eros)

25-28 scenes / 18 comprise love

Mist - no shape, depth, ignorance of surrounding life

Issue of Social Justice !

Topography of city – circularity of Inferno — Dante's
quest in the city

    Prison – A, B, C
    Match Factory A, B, C
      Circles of streets

Control of City – social ordered world
    A, B, C   Social institutions
  Institutions, factories, law courts, meetings, com.

Prison → Drover's situation

Kay's Petition – Lake

Commissioner (in jungle)

Home Secretary

Conrad's Milly

(empty) newspaper office

Kay – Surrogate (empty)

Commissioner – Conrad – similar characteristics
  moves to Scoby, Washed Priest
    Juncture of sexual

Interpersonal relationships tie into each
  other and get swallowed up by the
machinery of society – like streets reflect
    same inner connections

Pathology in Conrad - responsible for Milly
Historical plea
Communists don't believe in themselves
or their theories

1 1934

If justice is underlined so is love / overt structure in
Greene Canon

THE Assistant Commissioner was careful of his appearance
before meeting men younger than himself. It gave him the
same kind of confidence as dressing for dinner had done in
eastern forests. He opened the cupboard door and brushed
his dark suit before the mirror, his narrow yellow face bent
close to the glass. Young men had certain savage qualities;
they moved quickly; they sometimes carried poisoned
weapons. He brushed slowly in rhythm with the plodding
jungle step of his mind. He said to his secretary: 'I've put
my telephone number on the desk. If there's anything
urgent ...' As usual before a sentence was finished he
became lost in the difficulties of expression. Slowly, with a
fateful accumulation of hesitant sounds, he hacked his way
forward. 'Er – urgent, you will please – er – ring up the
number, and – er – ask for me.' Bowler-hatted, umbrella
over the left arm, he passed down long passages lined with
little glass cells. Telephone bells rang, electric buzzers
whirred like cicadas along his route, but his thoughts stepped
carefully on, undeflected, undelayed, certainly unhurried.

By the time he reached the courtyard, he had decided that
he did not care for politics. In Northumberland Avenue he
said to himself that justice was not his business.

All round Trafalgar Square the lights sprang out, pricking
the clear grey autumn evening. The buses roared up Parliament Street and swung in a great circle. A policeman at
the corner of the avenue recognized the Assistant Commissioner and saluted him. The Assistant Commissioner
nodded and crossed carefully where the signs pointed. I've
got nothing to do with justice, he thought, my job is simply
to get the right man, and the cold washed air did not prevent

Arrangement, relationship, reciprocity
Designed for social justice in this
society

his thoughts going back to damp paths steaming in the heat under leaves like hairy hands. One pursued by this path and that, and only as a last resort, when there was no other means of ensuring a murderer's punishment, did one burn his village. Justice had nothing to do with the matter. One left justice to magistrates, to judges and juries, to members of Parliament, to the Home Secretary.

The Assistant Commissioner paused for a moment before a shop window in Pall Mall filled with carpets. One could not live long in the east without learning something about them. The Assistant Commissioner was interested, but he had no idea whether the colouring was beautiful or coarse, whether the pattern pleased or repelled; he was interested because he could apply certain formulas to determine whether the carpet had been made in the east. He satisfied himself, as far as he was able without touching, that the carpets were genuine before he went on to the Haymarket corner. It never occurred to him to buy one; in his flat he had a few rugs on hardwood floors. A newspaper poster caught his eye: 'Drover Appeal Result', and another further up the Haymarket, 'Bus-Man's Appeal: Result'. An opportunity for investigation occurred to him, and he bought a paper, asking the man whether any particular interest had been shown in the news that night. The man shook his head and pointed to his mouth; he was dumb and the Assistant Commissioner walked on, frowning a little.

From Piccadilly he turned up a side street. He was not a man to waste a walk, even to an appointment. Women were coming out of offices on the ground floors of the tall blank buildings. He paused before one number. There had been an agitation recently in the Sunday press over brothels in London, and the police were paying particular attention to a certain flat. The Assistant Commissioner pursed lips which frequent fevers had drained of colour and left dry and pale. He considered morality no more his business than politics.

8

Little battles (microcosmic of pain anguish

It was impossible to keep the brothels closed. They sprang up like mushrooms overnight in the most unlikely places. One, he knew, had existed for years next door to a most respectable club. If you had them watched, your police were bribed; it was much better to let them be. At the top of the Burlington Arcade he noticed two policemen and another stood outside the Galleries on the opposite side of the street. Vine Street was posting its men in a new way, and he made a mental note to get Bullen to ring up the Inspector.

He entered the Berkeley suspiciously; he liked his appointments either at Scotland Yard or a Minister's house, and he could not understand why he had been brought to a restaurant. The pale leaf colours, the sofas, and the mirrors which flashed back from every side his own lined and jaundiced face irritated him as much as a bowl of flowers on a desk.

'Dear Commissioner.' He saw the private secretary detach himself from two women. Tall, with round smooth features and ashen hair, he shone with publicity; he had the glamour and consciousness of innumerable photographs. His face was like the plate-glass window of an expensive shop. One could see, very clearly and to the best effect, a few selected objects: a silver casket, a volume of Voltaire exquisitely bound, a self-portrait by an advanced and fashionable Czechoslovakian. 'Dear Commissioner.' He greeted the older man again with amusement, patronage, frankness and guile, putting his hand on his arm and guiding him to a remote corner. 'A sherry?'

The Assistant Commissioner said slowly: 'I should like a whisky and – er – soda.' He felt suddenly old and dusty; as if he had just returned from one of his torrid tedious marches, with a man left dangling in the jungle for the birds to peck, to find at headquarters a young cool messenger from the Governor. The secretary said: 'The Minister's so sorry not to see you himself. It's the debate, you know, on licensing.

He can't leave the House for a minute. Frankly, I'm worried about him. He'll knock himself up. First the town planning, then the juvenile offenders, and now the licensing.'

The Assistant Commissioner did not listen; he had learnt to husband his hearing; he cast his mind back over the work of the afternoon. The morning's work had already been docketed in his mind while he ate his lunch from a tray in his room. First the report of the finger-print experts on Ruttledge's marks and the knowledge that all the work on the Paddington Trunk Case must be done over again; whoever had murdered Mrs Janet Crowle it wasn't Ruttledge; then the report on the new wireless invention; and the exhibits in the Streatham Common murder and rape which he had wished to examine personally, the handkerchief rusty with blood and the piece of matted hair and the cheap wool béret.

'It's a battlefield,' said the secretary. 'Back and forth into the lobby. I know for certain he had no tea.'

I shall go over the ground myself, the Assistant Commissioner thought. The photograph of the two wooden chairs and the pressed grass did not tell enough.

'I don't want him to break down now, with two clear years in sight. Of course at the Dissolution he'll get a peerage.'

The Assistant Commissioner brought his mind back with difficulty from the Streatham villas. 'It was – er – about Drover ...?' Somebody in another corner of the lounge began to laugh. 'My dear, it was divine. They tied the pram on top of the taxi and Michael –'

'Yes,' the secretary said, 'it was about Drover. Now that the appeal has failed, it all rests on the Home Secretary. The poor dear man is worried, very worried, and all on top too of the licensing.' The secretary's wide pale face glistened softly under the concealed lighting and he leant forward with an infinite suggestion of frankness, with an overwhelming effect of guile. 'To tell you the truth, he'd have been glad, he'd have been tremendously relieved, if the appeal had been allowed.'

'Impossible,' the Assistant Commissioner said, 'there was no possible – er – line that the Defence could – could take.'

'Exactly. I was in Court. The Minister, you see, thought that the L.C.J. might give some excuse for a reprieve. But there was nothing at all to get hold of.'

'The policeman died,' the Assistant Commissioner said stubbornly, 'we got the man.'

'But the Minister, you know, doesn't want the poor devil's blood. Nobody does. It was a political meeting. Everyone was excited. Drover thought the bobby was going to hit his wife. He had the knife in his pocket. That, of course, is the snag. Why did he carry the knife?'

'They all do,' the Assistant Commissioner said. 'Helps to scrape away oil, mud. Cut up bread and – er – cheese.'

'Have another whisky?'

'No, no, thank you.'

The private secretary laid a square white hand on the Assistant Commissioner's arm. 'You know we must help him. He's in the devil of a state.'

'Do you mean – Drover?'

'No, no. The Minister, of course. My dear chap, if you could have seen him this afternoon. The devils. They made him fight every inch of the way; the Local Option Clause; the Tied Houses. And he's never at his best when he misses his cup of tea. Really, you know, I could almost have wept. And I had to send him in a note that Drover's appeal had failed. We must help him, or he'll never get through the Session.'

'Anything that I can do,' the Assistant Commissioner began in an embarrassed way. He was embarrassed because he did not know what the devil it was all about. He was annoyed that the working of his mind should be blocked like this. The Drover case was over; the Paddington trunk case, the Streatham murder required all the thought he could give to them. He ought, he knew, to leave them to his subordinates in the Criminal Investigation Department, the specialists in finger-prints and blood tests, the detective-inspectors who could go through the routine of inquiry blindfold. But it was his weakness, though in the east, in the enervating heat, it had been his strength, that he could never leave his department alone.

The private secretary's amiability spread luxuriantly like a quickly-growing creeper. 'I knew we could rely on you.' He proceeded to put the matter into a Parliamentary nutshell; the antitheses and balancing clauses, the calculated touches of humour when he spoke of the Opposition, had as little meaning to the Assistant Commissioner as the jargon of an art critic. 'You mean,' he said, 'that the Home Secretary would like to reprieve him?'

'Ah,' the private secretary wailed softly, leaning back on the leaf-green sofa, dabbing gently again and again at an automatic lighter, 'how you simplify. The affair is more complex than that. But we can start from that basis – the Minister would like to reprieve. But, you see, there are the strikes.'

'The strikes?'

'The cotton workers are out, and the railwaymen may be out next week. Drover is a Communist. Will it be taken as a confession of weakness if we reprieve him?'

The Assistant Commissioner opened his mouth to speak; he wanted to affirm that politics were not his business, but the secretary forestalled him. 'And if we hang him, will that be regarded too as a confession of weakness? Will they imagine that we are afraid to be magnanimous?'

'They?' the Assistant Commissioner asked. 'Who are they?'

12

'The Communists.'

'Ten – er thousand members.'

'Yes, yes, officially, but every striker, while he is out, is a Red more or less. One doesn't trouble about shades.'

'But what can they do?'

The private secretary leant forward and remarked impressively: 'If resentment kept them out a week longer, if over-confidence kept them out a week longer, it would cost the country fifty million.' He tapped the Commissioner's knee. 'More taxes and we lose the next election. What happens then?'

The Assistant Commissioner did not answer. Stooping over the trampled grass on Streatham Common, he would not have raised his eyes to a pyrotechnic display at the Crystal Palace, however brightly the sky was lit by rockets. The private secretary laughed and said, again with a frankness which gave the impression of deep guile: 'No peerage for the Minister anyway. And no under-secretaryship for me.'

'I don't understand,' the Assistant Commissioner began. It was one of his favourite expressions; extraordinary the number of occasions on which he could apply it: on first nights; when discussing the latest novel; in a picture gallery; when faced with an example of corruption. But turning over in mind the woollen béret, noting the texture of the wool, the pattern of the crochet, he understood more than the most sensitive artist, noticed more than the most inquisitive woman.

'The Minister argued in this way. You, more than any other single man, have your fingers on London: the poorer parts in particular.'

The narrow yellow face showed no pleasure; the Assistant Commissioner loved accuracy. 'The poorer parts only. I don't – er understand *this* place.'

'Oh,' the secretary said with airy amusement, 'I can answer for this place. If you can answer for – shall we say

13

the docks, for Paddington, Notting Hill, and King's Cross, the suburbs, Balham and Streatham, the –'

'Streatham,' the Assistant Commissioner murmured, interrupting the secretary's shabby pageant.

'If during the next week you can send in a private report on what you think the effect of a reprieve or an execution would be –'

'I don't like it,' the Assistant Commissioner said with an unusual lack of hesitation.

'A personal favour, dear chap,' the private secretary pleaded, 'because he's so tired, so worried –'

'He's got the report of the case, the judge's notes.'

'But if you could see him now, fighting every inch of the way, local opinion, tied houses.'

'If he finds it hard to decide, he might see the man for himself.'

'Would that be possible? Not for the Minister, of course, he's far too busy with the licensing, but perhaps for me.' The secretary smiled and tapped his cigarette. 'He depends, you know, a good deal on my advice.' Modestly he held the Minister's dependence up under the wide concealed light as a whimsical curiosity, a quaintly ugly antique.

'I'll take you to the prison now if it would – er interest, help you.'

'Does that mean that you consent, that you'll let us know,' he dabbed again at his automatic lighter, 'what people think about it?'

Again the Assistant Commissioner corrected him: 'The poorer parts,' and again with a studied gesture towards the leaf-green sofas and the two women whom he had left and who now smiled at him from a far corner, the secretary answered for the Berkeley. 'Oh, I can speak for the rest.'

The Assistant Commissioner, digging blunt nails into the sofa and heaving himself upright, said sharply: 'Have you ever been inside a prison?'

'Never.'

'You will be – interested.' He watched the bland face with distaste: he distrusted any man who showed so little sign of employment. Light employment, 'half-time work', had no meaning for the Assistant Commissioner, throwing his whole shrewd slow mind into every detail of his duty, into a crocheted béret, a second-hand trunk, a park chair, a cloak-room ticket; nor did the men with whom he spent his days disguise the fact that they worked – worked seriously, with a sense of responsibility, to keep life in them – detectives, bus-drivers, pawnbrokers, thieves.

'Most interesting, I'm sure.'

He preferred the morbid watchers at the prison gates, waiting for the striking of the clock, the posting of the typed notice ('carried out in the presence of the Governor, the prison doctor . . .'). Shivering in winter with the early cold, in summer touched by the pale heatless sun, they were made aware of what it was that kept them safe behind their shop counters, in their walk from fishmonger to grocer: they knew something of the stones, the rope, and the lime ('The executioner was Pierpoint').

'I have never seen a murderer,' the private secretary said. 'As far as I know of course.'

Yes, the Assistant Commissioner thought, I prefer those others. He said: 'We can take a bus from the Ritz.' He did not see why the country should pay for a taxi in order to satisfy the private secretary's interest, or to help the Home Secretary to a decision which he should be able to reach without difficulty, all the papers being before him, including the judge's notes.

'I have a car just round the corner.'

Something worried the Assistant Commissioner. He stood hesitating on the threshold of Piccadilly. Something had been said which he did not understand, it belonged to an alien world, but it was his duty to understand, something about. . . . The lights were all lit, the shop girls crowded the pavement on the way to the Underground. 'What were they saying?' he asked, 'about a pram on – er a taxi?'

The secretary laughed. 'A pram – on a taxi – how can I tell?' He laughed so loudly that two shop girls turned small vivid faces towards him; a clerk in dark clothes, carrying an attaché case, halted suddenly and stared at them, watching the two men turn the corner, rolling the phrase over on his tongue: 'A pram on a taxi,' convinced that he would never forget the meaningless joke which had set the men laughing.

The secretary sat with his bowler hat upon his knees, his right arm through a rest, talking of this and that. The blinds clicked down in the windows of the Knightsbridge *modistes*, and the end of Sloane Street was lost in blue haze; in the King's Road furniture was being carried indoors for the night. 'But perhaps you don't read novels.' Over Battersea Bridge the gulls came sweeping down to the level of the glass, and the lights from the Embankment crossed the grey flow, touched two barges piled with paper, rested on the mud, and the stranded boats and the walls of the mill. 'It all depends, of course, on her husband.' The fish-and-chip shops were opening, and all down the Battersea Bridge Road and past Clapham Junction, through a wilderness of trams and second-hand clothes shops and public lavatories and evening institutes, the Assistant Commissioner wondered, as he often wondered, at the beauty of the young tinted faces. Their owners handed over pennies for packets of fried chips, they stood in queues for the cheapest seats at the cinemas, and through the dust and dark and degradation they giggled and chattered like birds. They were poor, they were overworked, they had no future, but they knew the right tilt of a béret, the correct shade of lipstick. 'I should so much prefer Oslo.' They are admirable, he thought, and as the car left the crowds and the tramlines, he was saddened for a moment

16

like a man leaving his home. Candahar Road, Khyber Terrace, Kabul Street, the Victorian villas wavered in the mist like a shaking of shakos in old imperial wars.

The car climbed a hill and crossed the railway line by an hotel. Turning, the beams of the head-lamps caught a few bare trees, and a sandpit where children played in the dark. The car followed a long straight road beside the cutting, and a train overtook them, tearing south, dropping sparks on the roof. The secretary nodded towards a dark mass across the line. 'Is that the prison?'

'A school for girls.'

The car turned again; a policeman opened the door of a blue box beside a public-house, and a red tongue of light flickered up a glass globe on the roof. They drove between an allotment and a nursery garden towards a gate twenty feet high and, behind a wall, the roofs of square buildings and a tall hexagonal tower. 'We are here,' the Assistant Commissioner said, and they both sat quiet for a moment in the car, while a train went by unseen past the allotments, and the nursery gardens. 'Odd to hear that in your cell,' the secretary said with a touch of gloom.

'They can tell the time by it,' the Assistant Commissioner said.

The gates slid softly open pushed by a warder along a metal run, then closed behind them. They were surrounded by stone and hard lamplight. Somewhere a great many men were singing. 'Block C's at a concert,' the chief warder explained, and passing the door of the hall, they heard the tinkle of a piano which had not been tuned for a long time. Up in the glass chamber at the top of the hexagonal tower warders walked to and fro.

'The Governor's at the concert,' the chief warder said.

'Don't disturb him. This gentleman wants to take a look at Drover.'

The chief warder turned his old benevolent eyes towards the secretary. 'Has the gentleman been here before?'

'No,' said the secretary. 'No. It's all very interesting.' In the hall a man's voice was droning rhythmically; the Assistant Commissioner caught the words, 'fold up our tents like the Arabs.'

The chief warder halted. 'Ah, that'll be Adams. He's a wonderful reciter. Real artistes we have here. Make a donkey weep some of 'em.'

'What did he do?' the secretary asked.

'Tried to cut somebody's throat or something silly of the sort,' the chief warder said kindly. 'Ah, but you listen to this one. He's a treat.' A baritone began to sing. Through the cold night air the Assistant Commissioner imagined for a moment that between the verses he could hear the footsteps of the warders pacing in the tower.

They walked on, and the chief warder, pointing at one great cube of stone after another, began to explain to the secretary the geography of the prison. 'That's Block A. The new prisoners all go there. If they behave themselves they get shifted to that one there, that's Block B. Block C, the one we passed, that's the highest grade. Of course if there's any complaint against them, they get shifted down. It's just like a school,' the warder said, raising his old kind eyes with an expression of reverence towards Block A.

'And what happens to them in Block C?' the secretary asked.

'They have certain privileges. Have as many library books as they want. And they have more butter with their bread.' A heavy hollow bell began to ring in the tower. 'Every man to his cell except Block C,' the warder explained.

'Certainly,' the secretary said, 'your school comparison was sound. And how long before they can reach Block C?'

'Some do it in a year,' the warder said.

A searchlight in the top of the tower moved slowly round the prison, picking out grey stone after grey stone, while the bell clanged and clanged. Then the bell stopped and the light went out, and after its brilliance the lamps at every corner, the lamps over every doorway lost for a moment their harshness. Shadows fell like earth from a tilted spade.

'Just like children,' the warder said. 'We look after 'em just like children. I don't suppose you had prisons like this out east, sir?'

'No,' said the Assistant Commissioner, 'not – er – quite like this.'

'You should see the bakeries,' the warder said to the secretary. 'Bake all our own bread. Beautiful sweet bread it is. The officers have just the same bread as the men.'

They walked on, their shoes tingling on the asphalt. 'See that? That's the Roman Catholic chapel. Then there's a synagogue and a C. of E. That shed there. See that? That's where they see visitors. Like telephone boxes; wire on one side, glass in front. When they want to see they look through the glass, and when they want to talk they speak through the wire. Cunning, ain't it? After a year, of course, if they've behaved well, we allow 'em to embrace. They can come right outside on them seats.'

'Humane, very humane,' the secretary said. The Assistant Commissioner nodded, his face yellower than ever in the lamplight. The old dispute between punishment and prevention had no meaning for him; he had nothing to do with prisons; when, as now, his mind was irritated by an unsympathetic companion, he was glad of the fact. His work was simply to preserve the existing order, and it made no odds to him whether justice condemned a man to live in a common cell in a small tropical prison, with only the space of floor he could cover with his body and the sun burning through the bars, or in a private cell in Block C with a table for library books and a sing-song once a week. He had seen men

19

happy in the common cell, flinging a dice for extra bread, singing when the warder turned his back, and he had heard that men sometimes went mad in English prisons.

'And that building there?' the secretary asked. 'What's that? Billiard room? gymnasium?'

'Execution shed,' said the warder, quickening his step, but brightening the next moment at the sight of another great barred cube of stone, 'and here we are at <u>Block A.</u> Do you want to speak to Drover, sir?'

Absurd breaks through

'No, no,' the secretary said. 'That wouldn't do. The Minister wouldn't like me to raise his hopes.'

The long empty passage lined with doors was not quite silent. It was filled with slow breathing. The sound sifted down from metal floor above metal floor gleaming with electricity. A warder's boots clanked on the steel steps as he wound his way above their heads to the top. The breathing fell on them, as they stood in the well of the building, like the dropping of soft mould.

'They have an hour for reading before lights out.'

They were buried not only under the breaths of four hundred men, but under the turning of leaves. The faint rustle, like stray mice, could be heard along the passage in which they stood; sometimes, very faintly, it came down to them from the next layer of cells ten feet above their heads, but four floors higher even the warder's boots were inaudible, climbing through the blue glare.

They passed down the hall into a second smaller one which had been long disused. Once, the warder said, juvenile offenders had been lodged there. On the table in the centre of the hall, where the children had fed, a few everlasting flowers withered in jam jars and gathered dust. Two cells at the far end had been knocked into one to house the condemned man and his pair of watchers.

Drover was not reading; they spied on him through a little

window the size of a postcard in the cell door. He was asleep upright on his chair, clenched hands hanging between his knees. He might have been sitting for his portrait in the grey loose unaccustomed clothes, seen at better advantage than half hidden by a bus's hood, but in his dreams he seemed to be in a bus still; a foot pressed the floor, the hands opened a little and twisted. Then his lids parted and his eyes appeared, like the clear blue sweets which children suck. He gave the effect of strength and stubbornness, of reliability and a gentle obtuseness. All his movements were gentle; when he picked up a book the large hands moved awkwardly, deprecatingly; they held the book for a while upside-down.

The secretary said: 'You know, I seem to know his face. I suppose he wasn't on Route 13?'

'No. 10A,' the warder said.

'I suppose he's a type,' the secretary murmured, and there passed through his mind a whole parade of large heavy-coated quiet men seated in glass cages, twisting a wheel a fraction this way, a fraction that, wrestling with it at sharp corners, in country lanes turning up their thumbs to other drivers homeward bound through the rain from Maidenhead.

'He's quiet,' the warder said, 'we try to cheer him up a bit but he don't rightly seem to know where he is. A bit stupid, I think. Some of his mates came and saw him the other day. He couldn't get it into his head at first that they couldn't hear if he spoke through the glass. Wanted to see an' speak at the same time. But he had precious little to say for himself anyway. Got a bit interested when he heard that 10A's route was being changed. No,' said the chief warder, shaking his head, 'he's not easy to know. Anyway, he'll have to change now he shares with two of us. If he don't get a bit matey, it'll be no better than a funeral.'

They walked back across the asphalt yard; the warders

paced up and down in the tower, and the grey-clothed men were coming out of the concert room and crossing to Block C. 'Has his wife been here?' the secretary asked.

'She's quiet too,' the warder said. 'They're a pair of them for quietness.'

'Poor woman,' said the secretary heavily, and his thoughts turned to Lady Collins, whose husband's name had been called on the Stock Exchange before he went to prison for five years, and to the quiet and darkness of the house in Montague Square with the shutters up and the caretaker answering the telephone calls. But the Assistant Commissioner thought of the gossip in the fish-and-chip shops, the kind neighbours, and the pain of Monday mornings with the washing for one hung out in the back garden, and the voices calling to and fro over the wooden fences. This was not the worst pain, hope and fear in a cell, visits from the Chaplain; he had a dim memory that someone had once mapped hell in circles, and as the searchlight swooped and touched and passed, and the bell ceased clanging for Block C to go to their cells, he thought, 'this is only the outer circle'. The great gate rolled back on its metal groove, and the car passed out. The secretary put his arm through the rest and said softly, with the chill of stone a little on his tongue: 'You'll tell us then, won't you, what people think, what effect . . .'

The man who tears paper patterns and the male soprano were performing before the pit queues, the shutters of the shops had all gone up, the prostitutes were moving west. The feature pictures had come on the second time at the super-cinemas, and the taxi ranks were melting and re-forming. In the Café Français in Little Compton Street a man at the counter served two coffees and sold a packet of 'Weights'. The match factory in Battersea pounded out the last ten thousand boxes, working overtime. The cars in the Oxford Street fun-fair rattled and bounced, and the evening papers

22

went to press for the last edition – 'The Streatham Rape and Murder. Latest Developments', 'Mr MacDonald Flies to Lossiemouth', 'Disarmament Conference Adjourns', 'Special Service for Footballers', 'Family of Insured Couple Draw £10,000. Insure Today'. At each station on the Outer Circle a train stopped every two minutes.

Prison, Factory, Newspaper ties all

Trajectories cross in London

Characters - circles of environment close around them

~~Freeze~~ Women are disappointed in sex

    - interiority becomes closer consciousness

Topography
    City → persons → interiority

Loneliness of Kay Rimmer - edge of life
    Milly -
    Surrogate
    Condor - absurdity of stocker + stocked
    Commissioner) job, only security, celibates
    Conrad)

Parameters have been set by perimeter

tram - construct of the mind

2

CONDER opened one of the sound-proof boxes on the top floor and closed the door. Immediately all the typewriters in the room became silent, the keys dropped as softly as feathers. The chief reporter sitting on his desk with his knees pressed under his chin was interrupted in mid-sentence: 'I was waiting at Winston's all the morning and when he came out with his head all bandaged up, he only said – ' On the floor below the leader-writers sat in little studies and smoked cigarettes and chewed toffee, held up for the right word, looking in dictionaries, leading public opinion. On the floor below, the sub-editors sat at long tables and ran their blue pencils over the copy, scrawled headlines on scraps of paper, screwed the whole bunch into a metal shell, and sent it hurtling with a whine and a rattle to the composing room.

'Central 2301.'

On the floor below the swing door turned and turned and the porter sat in his box asking: 'Have you an appointment?'; the rolls of paper were wheeled like marble monuments towards the machines which turned and turned spitting out the *Evening Watch* pressed and folded: 'Mr MacDonald Flies Home to Lossiemouth. Are you Insured?', packing them up in piles of a hundred, spinning them down a steel incline, through a patch of darkness, into the waiting van.

'Press Bureau, please.'

A messenger scurried upstairs from the sub-editors' room to the leader-writers, from the leader-writers to the investigation department: 'Where is Topolobampo?' In the reporters' room the typewriter keys fell noiselessly, the chief

24

reporter sat on his desk, while his mouth opened and shut, Conder's breath misted the cold glass.

'Yes, this is Conder. Have you got any dope about the Streatham murder? Can't you invent something? Oh, well. No, the Chief's not much interested in Drover. What about Paddington? I suppose you are still clinging to Ruttledge. Not? Not sufficient evidence? You mean you've detained the wrong man again, I know you. There might be a leader in that if the Chief's had a bad lunch. Don't blame me. Yes, I shall trot along. Pink, very pink these days. Is it a good story? My missus likes me to be in bed by eleven. Oh, all right. The "Green Man" at 10.45. All the children send their love.'

Conder rang off and opened the door. The typewriters rattled like cavalry, and the chief reporter said: 'I asked her, "But what were you *doing* in his pyjamas?" ' Conder's face and his bald head gleamed softly in the lamplight. He said with habitual melancholy: 'Nothing doing at the Yard.'

'Nothing about Streatham?'

'No, and they've let Ruttledge go. He was the wrong man. They tried to give me a bromide about Drover.'

'The Chief's not interested in your Reds.'

'No. Can I go? I've got a party meeting this evening.'

'Feeling red?' the chief reporter asked with anxiety.

'Pink. Very pink,' said Conder in a low sad voice, his vitality visibly ebbing.

'We ought to get a line about Ruttledge into the final if we can. Trot it along to the stone and show it to the subs on the way.'

Conder took the lift to the floor below. It was quicker to walk, but for a few seconds, as he jerked downwards in the ancient metal cage, he was a captain of industry leaving his director's room in Imperial Chemicals. He stepped out and became again the successful journalist, the domesticated man with a devoted wife and six children to support, a

25

taxpayer, the backbone of the country. But his round shining face, his bald head, melancholy mouth and heavy lids never altered.

A man passed him in the corridor walking rapidly and called over his shoulder: 'Well, Conder, how are the Reds?' Conder nodded silently without a smile, Conder who was no longer the backbone of the country, but the hidden hand. Conder the revolutionary. But flick, flick, like the leaves of a book Conder's character turned and changed, and by the chief sub-editor's chair he was again the able journalist, the husband and the father. 'How are the kids, Conder?'

'I'm afraid of whooping cough. The youngest. They've had the doctor this afternoon. I shall know when I get home. Shall I try and get this Ruttledge par in under Streatham?'

'They may have to put it in the stop press. Is it worth a bill, d'you think, Conder?' and flick, flick, Conder was the man who knew the secrets of Scotland Yard, the crime reporter. But the same melancholy voice which spoke of whooping cough replied: 'Nothing to it.' In the composing-room the clerk asked him: 'How's the wife, Mr Conder?' while he searched the papers on his desk for the page plan, and at the stone the compositor, loosening the great slab of metal type to insert Conder's message, asked: 'And how does the new house suit you, Mr Conder?' For while they knew nothing of the captain of industry and laughed at the revolutionary and smiled in private at the intimate of Scotland Yard, they had accepted for ten years the family man, although he too was only one among the many impersonations of Conder's sad and unsatisfied brain. But it never occurred to him as strange that they should arbitrarily choose to recognize this as reality among all his unrealities, even during the few minutes of the day when he was the genuine Conder, an unmarried man with a collection of foreign coins, who lived in a bed-sitting-room in Little Compton Street.

'We are having trouble with the bathroom.'

'Ah.'

'How I envy you young unmarried men,' And it was true: Conder the married man with whooping cough in the new house and a defective bath and a wife who wanted him to be in bed at eleven envied the independence of the young compositor, envied it with such bitter knowledge of his own lot that in a few hours' time he would be himself young and independent, sowing his wild oats, twirling his umbrella down Piccadilly or across the Park, accosted by women, but they never got him beyond the doors of their flats, the entrances to their hotels, for on the threshold of enjoyment Conder, the revolutionary, whose vitality must not be weakened by enjoyment, or Conder, the married man, repelled him. Conder walked away along a passage which flashed with distorting mirrors.

*

The clock in the high tower struck six-thirty, and the siren cried through the dusk. No one responded; overtime was being worked in the match factory off Battersea Rise, but the siren, which was connected electrically with the clock, screamed on for a minute and a half while a hundred blue-and-white matchboxes jumped from the machines on to a great moving stair which drew them with slow solemnity, as if they were small coffins in a crematorium, to the blast of heat in the drying chamber. The hundred and fifty girls in the machine-room worked with the regularity of a blood beat; a hand to the left, a hand to the right, the pressure of a foot; a damp box flew out, turned in the air, and fell on the moving stair. It was impossible to hear the boxes falling, or a voice speaking, because of the noise of the machines, the machines in the hall, the machines in the cellar where tree trunks uncurled into thin strips of wood, the machines in the room above, where on a revolving band the pink-headed matches marched fifty deep up towards the ceiling, down towards the sulphur vats.

Kay Rimmer moved a hand to the left, a hand to the right, pressed down her foot, and winked her left eye. The girl opposite winked twice. Between the spitting of the machines, before the stair could move a foot away, the message passed. 'Hunting tonight?' 'No, the curse.'

Two men halted for a moment by the machines; a mouth opened in a shriek which could be heard as a faint whisper: 'From here to the drying,' but the last word was buried by the crash of sound too deep for recognition. The manager and the visitor passed out of sight, and the eyebrows flashed messages up and down the machines. 'Would you have him?' 'Not if he paid me.'

A hand to the left, a hand to the right, the pressure of a foot.

In the courtyard the manager pointed. 'That's Block A. The new employees go there for the simplest processes. Then if they work well they move to Block B, and so to Block C. Everyone in Block C is a skilled employee. Any serious mistake and they are moved back to Block B.'

'I suppose they have more pay,' the visitor said.

'And other privileges. A quarter of an hour longer at lunch time. The use of the concert-room.'

A hand to the left, a hand to the right, a pressure of the foot. All down the machine-room in Block C the eyelids flickered up and down; silent conversations passing with ease the barrier of noise. 'Pictures?' 'How's your boy?' 'I'm going out tonight.' A hundred and fifty match-boxes were carried towards the drying chamber.

'Beautiful food in the canteen. The same food is served to the management.'

'Millions of match-boxes a month,' the visitor said. 'It's wonderful when you think of it.'

'We even have our own hospital. Of course, there are

accidents occasionally . One can't avoid them. Carelessness or stupidity ...'

A hand to the left, a hand to the right, the foot pressed down. A finger sliced off so cleanly at the knuckle that it might never have been, a foot crushed between opposed revolving wheels. 'It never hurt her. She suffered nothing. Fainted at the sight of the blood.' 'So brave. She chatted all the way, carried on the stretcher to the operating-room.' Sickness benefit; half wages; incapacity; the management regrets. Between the line of machines the girls stood with tinted lips and waved hair, fluttering an eyelid, unable to talk because of the noise, thinking of boys and pictures and film stars: Norma, Greta, Marlene, Kay. Between death and disfigurement, unemployment and the streets, between the cog-wheels and the shafting, the girls stood, as the hands of the clock moved round from eight in the morning until one (milk and biscuits at eleven) and then the long drag to six.

Two hundred match-boxes moved upwards to the drying-room; the hands of the clock pointed to five minutes to seven. Greta put a hand to the left, Norma a hand to the right, Marlene pressed down her foot, Kay Rimmer tried to draw her own image in the dusty stale air, head tilted with a lazy sensuous faint desire, orange lips a little parted. The clock struck and every machine was immediately stilled. The matches fifty deep stayed in mid circle, the electric lights flickered to half strength, and the girls ran to the entrance and the stairs. Each employee in Block C had earned ninepence overtime.

In the cloakroom Norma put on her hat, Greta brushed her hair, Marlene made up her face. Norma said: 'Where are you going tonight, Kay?'

'Party meeting,' Kay said.

'How filthy,' Greta said. Kay Rimmer smiled. She could afford to smile; she was going where there would be fifty men to every woman; Greta would spend the evening with one boy at a cinema, Norma at a church meeting with a few pale men from a choir; art, politics, the church, Kay Rimmer had tried them all.

'You'll never meet anyone at those meetings,' Norma said. Kay Rimmer tested the name 'Jules' on her tongue. All down the long passage to the gate, with a confident unconscious smile, she let fall a succession of names, Terry, Herbert, Arthur, Joe; she welcomed the sound of any man's name with happiness, curiosity, and a profound ignorance. Peter, Bill, Ginger, Frank.

The name DROVER in great letters faced her from a poster at the gates and happiness, excitement and expectation left her; the name of the man she had seen for three years at every breakfast as he cut the loaf of bread or stirred his cup of tea, the man her sister had married, blew out at her from the crumpled paper. She read the poster twice: 'Drover's Appeal Fails.' I ought to go back to Milly, she thought. I oughtn't to go to the meeting. Peter, Bill, Ginger, Frank. She stood on the pavement and rubbed the kerb with her foot. Terry, Herbert, Arthur, Joe. She had met them all with Drover. I must go home. Milly will be desperate. But another name fell into the balance, 'Mr Surrogate'.

Milly never liked Jim taking me to the meetings. Milly loved him. Milly was jealous. A cold wind swept the pavement, bearing a scrap of silver paper from a chocolate box across the lamplight. Milly loved him Kay Rimmer hugged herself for warmth and thought of love, her orange lips parted, her sister's misery fighting in her face with excitement, expectation, the touch of a man in darkness. Of course I must go home, but she dropped the last name, 'Jules', softly and secretively.

In the shop windows where a light still burned, her face, as she quickly passed, was momentarily reflected across the bedroom slippers and the ready-cooked meats, fierce in the defence of happiness. There was ferocity even in her tread, light and quick, like an animal pacing the cave-mouth in protection of its young. Milly loves him. But she flashed to the help of her happiness breathing with weak trust in the darkness. The poster means nothing at all. They'll reprieve him. He isn't a murderer.

At the end of the street a man was waiting; she thought at first, because he was in shadow, that he was a stranger. Then she thought that he might be Jules. When she was twenty yards away she recognized Jim Drover's brother. She watched him with enmity as he stood in his dark clothes, one thin hand holding an attaché case; she knew that he was waiting for her.

'You've seen it?'

'Yes.'

'Where are you going?'

'I've got a meeting, Conrad.' Hopelessly happiness cried to her, gaiety and amusement. She said weakly: 'I suppose I ought to go home.'

'Is Milly alone?'

'Yes.'

He said: 'I don't see why you need go home. I'll go. You don't know my brother as I did. Milly and I can talk.' He leant against a shop front and behind him she saw disappearing into a dim interior a long avenue of second-hand coats. 'I was at the court all day.' She looked at him quickly, for the thought had come to her: he is going to cry. People will stop and stare at us. But his face was no whiter than it always was; the nerves had twitched in just that way as long as she had known him. Pale, shabby, tightly strung, he had advanced from post to post in his insurance office with the bearing of a man waiting to be discharged. While she watched him she lost the sense of his words and she had no idea of his meaning when he said: 'A stupid joke.' He asked her: 'Have you got people to sign the petition?'

She repeated 'Petition' and he became nervously angry,

31

clasping his attaché case. 'Something's got to be done. There's to be a petition.'

She explained: 'But I couldn't ask people at the works. I couldn't let them know it was Milly's husband.' With pale asperity he prepared a dagger thrust: 'You won't do a little thing,' but her appearance daunted him. Behind her were all the machines of the factory. With orange lips and waved hair she fought their uniformity and grey steel, but she was as one with them as a frivolous dash of bright paint on a shafting. 'The manager wouldn't like it. He'd sack me when he got a chance.'

It was not cowardice but realism that spoke. 'What's the use of a dozen names? One must live. It's different with you.' She told him gently how different. He was a chief clerk, indispensable to the office; they couldn't just go out into the streets and get another chief clerk. 'Anyone can do my job. But you,' she considered the dark coat, the stiff collar, the old-young face, with pride and contempt, as much as to say, it's not everyone who could be like you, and it's not everyone who'd want to be, 'you've got brains.'

They flattened themselves against the shop to let the factory girls go by, and behind them the second-hand coats, the dingy blouses shook with the shopkeeper's approach. Conrad Drover said grudgingly. 'It's lucky someone's got the brains.' She could not have told from his voice how he longed that it might be someone else. Brains had only meant that he must work harder in the elementary school and suffer more at the secondary school than those born free of them. At night he could still hear the malicious chorus telling him that he was a favourite of the masters, mocking him for the pretentious name that his parents had fastened on him, like a badge of brains since birth. Brains, like a fierce heat, had turned the world to a desert round him, and across the sands in the occasional mirage he saw the stupid crowds, playing, laughing, and without thought enjoying the tenderness, the compassion, the companionship of love.

'Now tell me: do you want to buy a coat or a blouse or a pair of trousers? Fine plus-four suit for twenty-five shillings. You don't need to go to Savile Row to do your shopping.' The avenue of clothes still quivered behind him.

'No, no, Conrad Drover said. 'I don't want anything.'

'Well then, tell me: do you think it's fair blocking up my shop talking to your girl? I've got to make a living, haven't I? Well now, tell me . . .'

'Come away,' Kay said, but he stood hesitating while he wondered whether the dealer was right, it wasn't fair; he ought to buy a tie or a pair of socks, something cheap which he could afford.

'Oh, no. You wait a moment and tell me . . .'

'Shut your mouth,' Kay Rimmer said, taking Conrad by the arm and drawing him a little way down the street.

*

Sacrifice, Mr Surrogate thought, as he stared from the window of his bare and tasteful room into the wide blue pool of the Bloomsbury square. The plane trees spread pale palms in the lamplight, and the postman went knocking from door to door. Sacrifice. Mr Surrogate strode to the door and back again to the window, pausing for a moment at the mirror over the Adam mantel to catch himself warily unaware, plump and fair, his hair grey over the ears, his mouth a little too resolute. But he corrected that, self-conscious for a moment when he caught the insolent Tartar eyes of Lenin in the plaster bust. Comrades, one man must die for the people. We accept Comrade Drover's sacrifice, knowing, knowing – back to the window, a turn on the heel, and again the bourgeois face with its insolent stare.

There was a knock on the door. It was cautiously opened

and a hand slipped a letter through on to the sideboard. 'Thank you, Davis, thank you.'

'It's gone seven, sir.'

'Thank you, Davis, I am quite aware of the time.' Comrades, Mr Surrogate began again. Comrades, we must not be daunted; no sacrifice is too great. . . . He stopped again and regarded nervously the involved beautiful unintelligible handwriting. He opened the envelope reluctantly and deciphered with difficulty the invitation to dinner which lay, like a bare white egg, in an intricate oriental nest of lettering. Caroline is curious about Drover, he thought. He never gave the surface value to an invitation. At the heart of his elaborate conceit lay an extravagant humility.

His inclination was to refuse, but he knew that he would accept, that he would suffer the hours of martyrdom, sitting in front of his dead wife's pictures which hung on every wall, the exquisite stylized landscapes, the green populous vistas which had emerged so simply and certainly from her malicious cantankerous brain. During a long, faithful and unhappy marriage they had exposed each other to Caroline Bury with a complete lack of reticence, and now to visit Caroline was to expose himself again. 'Sacrifice.' There were occasions of brutal insight when she recognized the cause of his philosophy and his politics; his inability to conceal anything had humiliated him so often that he had needed to form a philosophy of humiliation, to found his career on self-exposure. 'Be humble that you may be exalted,' and from the depth of humility he would spring refreshed to the height of pride.

'Shall I whistle a taxi, sir?'

He called to his servant through the closed door, 'Can't you leave me alone, Davis? I can look after myself,' and twisting in the seesaw of pride and humility between the window and the door, between the mirror and the bust of Lenin, he heard his wife's voice saying with fierce dislike:

34

'You haven't practised that expression enough.' Suddenly through the stillness, like the ghost of old dinners, he heard a nut crack. He stayed very still, half expecting to smell the bouquet of port, to hear the clink of a glass, but there was a silence, except for the hiss of the gas fire, the faint rat-tat of the postman on the opposite side of the square. Not until he began to stride the room again was the sound repeated; it was unmistakably the cracking of a nut.

Mr Surrogate gazed at the glass bowl of cobnuts on the sideboard and then stealthily approached the bookcase. All along one shelf stood the record of his intellectual progress: *Forward to Free Trade, Back to Protection*, in their English and American editions; only with *The Capital Levy* had his writing reached the Continent and German and Czechoslovakian publishers. His eye followed with pride the record of his increasing humility: *The Nationalization of Industry, with An Appendix on Scales of Compensation* was followed by the brief triumphant title, *No Compensation*. The shelf was not quite full. The American edition of *The Dictatorship of the Worker* leant at an angle against the shelf end. Mr Surrogate stooped and put his ear against *The Capital Levy*; a nut cracked boisterously in the darkness behind.

Mr Surrogate spread his fingers and withdrew suddenly and simultaneously three editions of *No Compensation*. There, surprised in the act of dining, a nut between its paws, sat a mouse. Mr Surrogate and the mouse were both startled. For quite a long while they stared at each other without moving. The mouse did not even drop the nut. Perhaps it hoped to remain unnoticed. It may never have seen before a human face so close, almost within reach of an extended tail, and the great white moony expanse may have had the appearance of a natural phenomenon. All round it, and all along the bookcase, lay the débris of uncounted meals and worse, breadcrumbs, broken shells, scraps of old envelopes and of discarded manuscript, toffee papers, for Mr Surrogate had a sweet tooth. It had evidently dined nightly and dined well. Mr Surrogate cautiously drew back, and the mouse, dropping the nut, whisked into the darkness behind *The Capital Levy*.

With his hand already outstretched to rob it of that refuge, Mr Surrogate became compassionate. His whole face softened and relaxed. 'Poor little mouse.' His mouth fell a little open, and he yearned towards it in its shelter. 'Poor, poor little mouse.' He thought of the great Russian novelist comforted in the Siberian prison by the nightly visitation of a mouse. 'I too. The prison of this world,' and his eyes filled with tears, withdrawing from *The Capital Levy* to gaze through the window at the lamps and the plane trees. He went to the sideboard and found a little bit of cheese.

For some time the mouse resisted the temptation of the cheese. It obviously suspected Mr Surrogate's intentions. It lay so quiet behind *The Capital Levy* that Mr Surrogate feared that it had escaped to a hole. He began to feel irritated by a mouse. He withdrew the cheese and toasted it for a moment before the gas fire.

The smell of the toasted cheese had an immediate effect. The mouse emerged, picked up the cheese, and disappeared behind *The Capital Levy*. It had a shiny satin rump and an air of great respectability. One expected a bunch of keys to dangle at the waist; but it preferred to eat in private, in the housekeeper's room. Mr Surrogate did not fetch another piece of cheese; he was no longer compassionate; the tedium of Siberia came terribly home to him when he thought of anyone depending for amusement on a mouse. The clock struck a quarter to seven.

'Davis, fetch a taxi. I shall be late.'

Mr Surrogate found his hat and looked back once from the door. The mouse was still in hiding. It had nibbled a corner off *The Dictatorship of the Worker*, and it had certainly not used the bookshelf only for meals. 'Davis,' Mr Surrogate said, 'set a mousetrap by the bookcase.'

*

Jules Briton dried his hands on the towel which hung behind the counter and warmed them close to the great copper urn. A French prostitute leant on the counter and talked to him; she had left her beat in Lisle Street to swallow some coffee. Jules answered in good careful uneasy French; so long as his mother was alive he had been allowed to speak nothing but English, for she had borne a grudge against her husband, who had left her with a bankrupt business and disappeared to his native country. Jules had never been to France, but his mother had beaten into him with a hard English rectitude the idea of something shameful, irresponsible, and at night, when, under the influence of drink, she moaned for lost love, beautifully gay. France meant the women in pairs trudging up Wardour Street and down again, the false coins slipped into the cigarette machine, Mass in the dim, badly decorated L'Eglise de Notre Dame, French illustrations, French postcards, French letters. It had the furtiveness of lust, the sombreness of religion, the gaiety of stolen cigarettes.

The café door opened, and Jules fluttered a hand to Conder advancing through the steam. 'I've got something good for you,' he said.

'Come upstairs then,' Conder said. Conder's bed-sitting-room was on the first floor. On the wall hung a picture of the royal family taken before the war, the King, the Queen, a crowd of unidentifiable scared children in sailor suits, a princess with frizzy protuberant hair and a large bow. 'Well,' Conder said, 'what is it?'

'A paper rouble,' Jules said. He spread it out on the eider-down.

'How did you get it?'

'Found it on the floor when I was sweeping up.'

'Well, that is good, that really is good,' Conder said, standing back and gazing at it, passing one hand across his bald head. 'I never expected to get a rouble. They aren't allowed to take them out of the country, you know. I shouldn't be a bit surprised if that was worth – well, a couple of shillings. To a collector, of course.' He fetched a tin box, which had once been used for chocolate biscuits, from the drawer of his table and turned the contents out on the bed beside the rouble note. Whenever he acquired a new coin or a new note he examined the old ones. 'That's pretty, that Australian shilling. And those Greek lepta. This Turkish one I got on a bus. I could tell extraordinary stories of what I've picked up on buses.' He handled the coins tenderly, rubbing them with his handkerchief, flattening out the creases in the notes. Outlandish names tripped off his tongue – taels, libras, pengos, schillings, zlotys and santims, piastres, annas and lats, centavos and sens.

Jules looked in Conder's shaving mirror and then at a copper coin. 'I think, you know, I am very like Napoleon III. If I grew a little beard . . .'

'I've got a full set now of these Irish coins,' Conder said.

'An Imperial.'

'This pig.'

Jules' mind wandered from the Emperor to Sedan, from Sedan to Paris, from Paris to the Commune.

'Are you going to the party meeting? We ought to be off.'

'A symbolic figure representing Plenty.'

'Conder,' Jules said, 'what's happened about Drover?'

'Appeal dismissed. A Sower and a Plough.'

'I know his wife's sister.'

'A symbolic figure representing Peace.'

Conder laid the coin carefully with the others on the flowered eiderdown. 'Did you say you know his wife?'

'Her sister. They live together.'

'I might get an interview out of that,' Conder said with faint interest.

'She'll be at the meeting,' Jules said.

Conder looked at his watch. 'We'd better be off.' The brief exhilaration of the collector had left him; he was a journalist again dissatisfied with his pay, his profession and life.

'Will they hang him?'

'One can't tell,' Conder said. A journalist was supposed to understand the working of the world, but Conder had spent his life in learning the incomprehensibility of those who judged and pardoned, rewarded and punished. The world, he thought, as they walked between the coffee-stalls, past the lit restaurants, the foreign newspaper shops, and the open doorways, was run by the whims of a few men, the whims of a politician, a journalist, a bishop and a policeman. They hanged this man and pardoned that; one embezzler was in prison, but other men of the same kind were sent to Parliament. Conder, the revolutionary, became a little flushed with the injustice of it, but he knew well enough that it was not systematic enough to be called injustice.

'I hope they don't hang him. He used to come to meetings sometimes. He never spoke.'

'You should ask the Bishop of London.'

'How can he know?'

'He's as likely to know as anyone.'

'Isn't it any good doing anything? Petitions? Anything?'

'That's just the thing. You can't tell. Petitions have been signed for every murderer who's ever been hung. Good simple people will sign a petition for anyone. This Streatham rape and murder. When the man's caught hundreds of women in Streatham will sign a petition for him.'

'Then it's no good. It can't have an effect.'

'Ah, but you can't tell. Once in fifty times it has an effect.

The minister picks up the papers and sees a name he knows. It may be only the name and not the man at all, but it makes him look again and think a bit. Or he's just spoken to a big meeting and been cheered, and then he feels democratic and that the people know best. Or he's had a good dinner. Perhaps he's drunk too much. Perhaps he's the one minister in twenty years who drinks too much. But it makes the difference. You can't tell. You've got to try. None of us knows what motives they may have for hanging Drover or for reprieving him. Politics and religion are all mixed up in it.'

— They turned into the darkness and quiet of Charlotte Street. The policeman at the next corner watched them approach with cynical amusement. Jules said suddenly, 'We are playing at this.'

'Playing at what?'

'Being Reds.'

A saloon car with a high yapping horn tore by them, shattering the street with the brilliance of its headlights, so that doorways and shop-fronts and newsagents' posters sprang out and receded. The car took the corner in a wide skid and disappeared in the direction of King's Cross. The policeman at the corner saluted. 'Who was that?' Jules asked. He had caught sight as the car passed of a lit interior packed tight with large men in soft hats, sitting in two rows, staring at each other without speaking.

'The Flying Squad,' Conder said.

Jules thought of their silence and of the talk to which he was going. Men would be making speeches to a late hour, reconstructing England in theory, abolishing poverty on paper. He felt sullen and dissatisfied as he turned the corner by the policeman and met the man's amused glance. He wanted something he could follow with passion, but Communism was talk and never action, and patriotism puzzled him; he was not English and France meant nothing but holy statues and Napoleon III, prostitutes and stolen cigarettes. He wanted someone to say to him: 'Do this. Do that. Go here. Go there.' He wanted to be saved from the counter and the tea urn, the 'Weights', and the heartless flippancy of the café.

'Will something be done about Drover tonight?'

'Surrogate will speak, I expect, and Bennett. There may be a delegate from the garage.'

He would have dedicated himself to any cause, any individual, even a woman, if he could have been given a motive to be as serious as those six policemen driving down Charlotte Street.

'This girl,' Conder said, 'Drover's sister –'

'His wife's sister.'

'Is she pretty?'

Jules nodded. Nothing satisfied him that evening. Kay's pretty, he told himself with depression, and amiable and light as myself.

They were late at the meeting, and as they passed through the unlit vestibule, past the empty booking office, they could hear snatches of a speech. The dreary syllables rose and fell like tired feet. All through the hall one heard the tread of hunger marchers; the ugly makeshift banners dipped and fell in the hopeless rioting of innumerable Red Sundays. Jules was moved by the sincerity of the thousands who did not wrangle for leadership, who were ready to follow in patience and poverty. Three rows in front he saw Kay Rimmer crying with her head in her hands. He whispered to Conder: 'We must save Drover. Somehow. There are thousands of us.' Until the next speech began he thought that he had found the cause he wanted.

'There is no one here,' Mr Surrogate said, 'who would not gladly now change places wth Comrade Drover, no one so vile who would not with a joyful heart have struck the same

41

blow against capitalist oppression.' At the sound of his own voice realities receded like the tides; he had no picture in his mind of the condemned cell, the mask, the walk to the shed; he saw Caesar fall and heard Brutus speak. He called out with a breaking voice across the tip-up seats and the green faces, over the disused cinema, to Antony standing against the furthest wall: 'Who is here so base that would be a bondman? If any, speak; for him have I offended.' Somewhere in the shadows a girl was weeping and Mr Surrogate called again through the streets of imperial Rome: 'There is no cause for grief. Every faith demands its sacrifice. When Drover dies, the Communist Party in Great Britain will come of age.' The intellectual in the horn-rimmed glasses said, 'Hear! Hear!' and clapped.

A man called Bennett asked: 'What measures are being taken?'

Mr Surrogate raised his hand. 'I was coming to that. I am not on the executive committee of the party. I am trying to speak for the ordinary member. I propose that a collection be taken on the spot in aid of Comrade Drover's widow and that a proportion of the collection recently held in London for the fighting fund be allocated to a suitable memorial.'

Bennett said: 'He's not dead yet.'

'We can't disguise from ourselves,' Mr Surrogate said, 'that there's little hope. The petition sheets, of course, will be handed to everyone as he goes out.'

A man in a heavy overcoat stood up. 'I've been asked to come 'ere,' he said, 'by the garidge. Couldn't we pass some sort of resolution now, on the spot, askin' Parliament . . .'

The horn-rimmed intellectual rose beside Mr Surrogate. 'Quite impossible,' he said. 'Quite impossible. We are more than ten persons. By 13 Charles 2, Stat. 1, we should all be liable to imprisonment. It's out of the question.'

'Sit down,' Bennett called, and Mr Surrogate and the man

42

from the garage sat down hastily. 'Sit down,' Bennet repeated.

The treasurer said: 'I'm not taking my orders from you, Comrade Bennett. If the meeting – '

'Sit down.'

Mr Surrogate crouched over his shoe-lace. He was wondering bitterly whether all movements ended in a scrimmage of individuals for leadership. He thought of the first Fabian Society, of the ladies in their Walter Crane dresses and shorn heads and cigarettes, their belief in the perfectibility of the human character, and their patronage of house painters and plumbers. He remembered the arguments at midnight going home over Chelsea Bridge in a hansom with a chosen companion.

'Now,' Bennett's voice said above him, 'we can get on to business.' Mr Surrogate looked up and away. He knew only too well his mind's trick of remembering causes in human terms: the Fabian Society in terms of that midnight hansom and the first tentative pure-minded discussions of Free Love and the Emancipation of Women with a girl who would not be serious even when she was in bed with him.

'Or is there any other intellectual who wants to 'ear' is own voice?' Bennett continued with his eyes on Mr Surrogate; but Mr Surrogate looked away in deep despair. For years now, passing through every stage of socialism, he had believed with complete sincerity that he would one day get into touch with the worker; but the plumber who had written a Fabian Essay was the man of that class he had known most intimately. He was the only one, an elderly man with steel spectacles and a background of religion and hedge schooling, who had been wholly serious, who could bandy back and forth with Mr Surrogate the abstractions he loved: Social Betterment, the Equality of Opportunity, the Means of Production.

Personalities! Mr Surrogate shuddered. They had always betrayed him. Women whom he had wished to emancipate flirted with him, and when the lovely abstractions of Communism had lured him into the party – Comradeship, Proletariat, Ideology – he found there only Bennett. He resented even Drover's intrusion as an individual to be saved and not a sacrifice to be decked for the altar. In a cause was exhilaration, exaltation, a sense of Freedom; individuals gave pain by their brutality, their malice, their lack of understanding. He could live in a world of religions, of political parties and economic creeds; he would go mad rubbing shoulders at every turn with saviours, politicians, poor people begging bread. And yet he could not be happy alone among his glamorous abstractions; he wanted a companion to help to confirm his belief that these things were real – Capitalism and Socialism, Wealth and Poverty – and not these other things, champagne and charity balls and women bearing their twelfth child in an overcrowded room.

'Is that girl here?' Conder asked.

Jules said: 'We'll catch her after this.'

'There's a story here for the morning papers,' Conder said, 'but how can I use it? My faith to the party would be broken.' He ran his hand distractedly over his bald head, talking on in a low voice, listening to what Bennett was saying, thinking of several things at once. Drover's wife, there might be a good interview, 'not sit down under it like bloody intellectuals,' suppose there are other newspaper men here, 'pamphlet 36', mustn't risk being thrown out of the party, if it's in the morning papers I shall be blamed, 'three volunteers to distribute at the gates,' I shall be blamed, I shall be blamed.

'I'm a delegate from the garidge. They want to know what's going to be done about Drover.'

'I'm coming to Drover all in good time,' Bennett said.

'There'll be the petition to sign. Do you expect us to attack the prison? What's the good of breaking windows? If they want to 'ang 'im, they'll 'ang 'im.'

'There's a lot of feeling at the garidge.'

'Then 'old a meeting at the garidge. Get some of the intellectuals to talk till you feel all right. I've got up 'ere to face facts.'

'Something ought to be done.'

'This meeting's got more to attend to than Drover. Who's Drover anyway? I've never 'eard 'im do anything for the party. We've got a big job on now that can't wait for Drover.'

Somebody in the middle of the hall called out: 'Good old Bennett,' and everybody laughed.

'They're shouting Drover this and Drover that at me. Drover doesn't matter now. It's not one policeman we want to kill. I'm not a talker. I'm the man who does a job. We've got enough blacklegs. We've got 'em in the party, we've got 'em in this 'all as like as not. Spies and blacklegs. Men who've never done a stroke of honest work, talkers, scribblers. We've got to weed 'em out.'

'Really,' Conder said, stroking his head, 'he's going too far. He's questioning our honesty.'

Kay Rimmer sat with her head on her hands and her eyes on the floor. She thought of the long streets between her and Battersea, the Jews in Charing Cross Road, the whores in Coventry Street, and the long hill of Piccadilly; at the other end, past the King's Road and the cabmen's shelters, past the slow dull river and the warehouses and the tram-lines, Milly waited, Milly with her intolerable grief, fear in the kitchen, suspense in the sitting-room, pain on every stair. 'They're shouting Drover this and Drover that at me.' Drover who had never intruded, who had sat as quietly as a visitor in his own home, importuned now from every

45

piece: the plant unwatered, because it had been his job, no beer in the house because he used to fetch it. I want to enjoy myself, she thought, Jim doesn't matter to me, I could hate Milly for this, and looking up she saw Mr Surrogate's smooth cheek and pale hair.

'There's Kay,' Jules said and waved his hand. He noticed again that she had been crying. Above his head Bennett rumbled on. His rage was like a storm which, if two were together in a room, drew them together with its darkness and the closeness of the air. He allowed himself for a while to think of loving Kay; she was more of an individual with her eyes wet. His mind, which had been misty with regret, vague with aspiration, cleared momentarily, and it occurred to him that possibly all he needed was a woman. Love when one had no money was a chancy thing; one took it when it came, but that was seldom. They were always, women, wanting something in return: a visit to a dance hall, chocolates, a cinema; they thought it undignified to take the pleasure as its own reward; or else they became moony, passionately mono-gamous, and when he wanted to laugh and love and make a noise, they wanted to be quiet in the dark, alone with him. But Kay was not like that; she had too many friends ever to want to creep into corners; he almost believed that it would be safe to love her. Her tears did not frighten him; they meant that she would be glad of company; he got miserable himself when he was left alone, would have paid anything he had for even Conder's company, was lost, was frightened. Only a woman, only a noise, only a gramophone playing or people talking could save him then from sinking back, back into himself, meeting his harsh mother on the threshold, back past the moaning drunken cries, back past the quarrels in the next room, back to the kisses and the sweets and early bed, back to no more being. Shout, sing, be in a crowd as he was here; that was better than searching in the dark for something as hopelessly gone as the sheltered existence of the womb. 'Jules, you have forgotten this. . . . Jules, you have forgotten that. . . . God damn you, how much longer have I got to wait?' Slowly he would emerge, apologize, explain. They thought, all the employers and the customers he had to deal with, that he was lazy, but he forgot as easily his own affairs, his handkerchief, his coat when it was stormy, and today the letter which had come for him, addressed and re-addressed with a French stamp, only this moment remembered. 'I'll open it at lunch-time,' but at lunch-time a hurdy-gurdy was turning in the street, two children were circling with raised pinafores, an unemployed man was slapping his hands to help them with the time, and Jules could stand and laugh and gossip, feel himself for ten minutes part of the street, part of London, part of a country, not one abandoned by his mother's death to fight his way in a land which was his only by the accident of birth.

The surface of the brain was aware of Bennett talking, Mr Surrogate bending his head over his shoe, Kay trying to catch his eye; their images danced across his brain like rain on glass, leaving no impression. He was already away, seeking what he had lost, what he was never quite reconciled to losing, complete dependence, a definite object (to breathe, to grow, to be born), the impossibility of loneliness.

'Come on,' Conder said, 'it's over. I knew they'd do nothing about Drover. They're good for nothing but talk.'

'Why do you come?' Jules asked.

They were pushed together for a moment in the entrance, somebody thrust petition papers into their hands, and they were again apart with a foot of pavement and a splash of lamplight between them. Something in that quick involuntary contact affected Conder; it was as when one shared a taxi with a strange woman after a party and the chance contact induced confidences between a street and a street.

47

'I suppose,' he said, 'when everything is badly wrong, even the talk of something better. . . .' He looked at Jules sideways, with shame, with a sharp hopefulness.

The street was full of people, laughing and going home. Jules longed to be with them. He said to Conder: 'There's Kay,' and to Kay: 'This is Conder.' Conder took off his hat and Kay's eyes rested with distress, boredom, a veiled malevolence on the bald head.

'Can we see you home?' Conder asked.

'But I don't want to go home yet,' Kay said. 'It's early.' She leant against the lamp-post and pressed her cheek against the iron.

'Come to the park then,' Jules said.

'It'll be cold.'

'A café.'

'Both of you come with me,' Conder said, 'and have a drink at the "Fitzroy".'

'I've had too many drinks at the "Fitzroy". Can't you suggest something new, something exciting?'

Conder put his hand to his head. 'I'd ask you to come and have some supper, but you see I've got to meet someone at 10.45.' She smiled with unbelief. Men couldn't even think of a new excuse.

'We could go to a cinema for an hour,' Jules said.

'I don't want to go to a cinema or a café or a pub, and I don't want to go home and I don't want to walk about in the park.' The men stood round her with perplexed irritated faces. They ought to understand, she thought, what home will be like with Milly waiting there, not sleeping, not taking off her clothes, hopelessly entangled with a man who is not there, who will never be there again. She wondered with a kind of vexed sensuality what it felt like to be so tied to a man. These were men, standing round her offering coffee and beer and moving pictures, and never dreaming – you could tell from the dull depressed faces – that the only thing she wanted now, this minute, this night, was the knowledge of what it felt to be so tied to a man.

Jules said: 'It's nearly 10.45, Conder, now.'

She gazed from one to the other of them, from Conder, short, shabby, with a bald head and ink-stained fingers, and nails blunt from a typewriter, to Jules with the lost look she told herself it would be easy to love.

'Won't anybody say something funny? I want to laugh.' She knew suddenly that Jules understood, that if Conder had not been there, he would have made love to her, but this knowledge irritated her and when Conder looked at his watch and said, 'Yes, really. I must be off,' she exerted all her charms to keep Conder, smiling and pouting, a faint evocation of a famous film actress in a small part in an early faded film. 'Oh, but I know you just aren't interested in me. You've not really got an appointment.'

'Believe me, Miss Kay,' Conder said, 'there's no one I'd rather stay and talk to, and I hope that you'll let me call around at the works and take you out to lunch one day. If it wasn't so important –'

'What is it anyway?'

'Ah, but ladies can't keep secrets,' Conder said, bowing impressively. His personalities flickered so quickly that he was himself confused, uncertain whether he was the revolutionary, the intimate of Scotland Yard, or, a new part this, the master spy. He took off his hat and moved quickly round the corner into Charlotte Street, head a little bent, butting against the cold sweep of the wind.

'Kay,' Jules said.

'Look,' she said quickly, 'there's Mr Surrogate.' Mr Surrogate came out of the cinema alone, paler than when he entered. He had shut himself into a lavatory until he thought the place was clear, for he was unwilling to encounter Bennett. It would arouse bad feeling, he told himself, the party mustn't be split into groups; and at intervals, hearing feet

49

prowling round the wash-basins, he had pulled the chain convincingly. His face clouded when he heard his name spoken, but it cleared again at the sight of a girl under the lamp-post. He padded deprecatingly across the pavement. It was quite like the old days of the Fabian Society. 'Well, Comrade? What about a cup of coffee?' He looked at her more closely. 'You are the girl who cried.'

'Jim Drover's my brother-in-law.'

Mr Surrogate was taken aback. Drover was a sacrifice, Drover was a comrade, on Drover's death the British Communist Party would come of age. 'I'm sorry,' he said. He felt rattled and betrayed by the individuality of men.

'You needn't for me,' she said. 'It's my sister who's hurt. I hoped I'd have some news for her. I don't want to go home and say there's nothing going to be done.'

'The party can do nothing,' Mr Surrogate said.

'I'm afraid of what Milly will do. She's a quiet one. You don't know what she's thinking. But I know they were happy. They were so dull together, they couldn't be anything else but happy.' Mr Surrogate nearly called to her to stop. Pain was unbearable to him. His nerves shrank from it. He remembered with longing the bare panelled walls of his flat, the glow of the gas fire, the mirror and the Adam mantel. Only one suffering individual penetrated there, and she was dead and could be dismissed and forgotten with a book.

'They'd been married five years.'

'Listen,' Mr Surrogate said, 'there's still the petition.'

'She doesn't believe in that.'

'There are things one can do – privately. People one can see. I'll speak to Caroline Bury.'

'If only there was something I could tell Milly.'

'There shall be, I promise you.' Somehow the promise of the evening must be re-established, drawn away from

suffering. 'Come back with me now and we'll discuss it.'
'Shall I?'

'Go along, Kay,' Jules said. He hoped that Mr Surrogate
would invite him to go with them; he too wanted to do
something for Drover; he would enjoy a party instead of
bed, a little drink, a lot of talk, and after they had discussed
what to do, a little music. But his encouragement angered
Kay. 'It's too late,' she said.

Mr Surrogate was taken aback; he had forgotten in his
resistance to pain that she was a girl, someone with whom he
could discuss the old burning question of the Emancipation
of Women. 'These bourgeois ideas,' he said. 'I'm surprised.'
He waved to a taxi.

*

Conder opened the smoking-room door; in a corner the genteel woman in black velvet sat as usual beside a table of
bottles. Over the fireplace hung a photograph of an admiral
with a blasé face and a tilted cap; a plaque on the walls
stated that a naval officers' club had met in the room between 1914 and 1918.

'Anyone asked for me?' Conder asked.

'No, Mr Simpson's not been in tonight, nor Mr Barham,
Mr Conder. We've been quite quiet.' Her genteel voice made
the words sound like 'quack, quack'.

'I'll look in the bar.' Conder went downstairs. But he did
not open the bar door, for through the glass he saw Bennett.
His back was turned and he had lifted a glass of bitter to his
lips. His friends crowded the bar and the noise of their
laughter peopled the stair, so that Conder stood for a
moment very still, feeling himself the centre of a hostile
crowd. The outer door opened, and a large man in a soft hat
came in; he wore ordinary clothes like a disguise. 'Hallo, Mr
Conder,' he said. Conder jerked his finger to his lips. 'Shsh,'
he said, and retreated up the stairs. 'Shsh.' The large man

followed him; he took a long look into the bar on the way. 'What's got you?' he said.

'I'll tell you in a moment. Have a drink? You're late.'

'How nice to see a new face,' the woman in black velvet said.

'Two Basses,' Conder said. The woman trailed back to her corner, an empty bottle in either hand, with the manners of an Edwardian hostess.

'What's got you?' the man said, and raising his glass, 'Here's how.'

'Look here, Patmore,' Conder said, 'you may get me into trouble. Bennett's downstairs. He's spoiling for trouble. If he saw me with you – '

'Why, Mr Conder, can't you entertain a friend?'

'There are only two things, Patmore, you could possibly be, one's a policeman and the other's a bailiff.' The thought of Bennett in the bar frightened and irritated him. 'I'm tired to death, Patmore, of you fellows at Scotland Yard. You're a lot of ostriches burying your heads in the sand, thinking you aren't noticed. You've released Ruttledge. You haven't an idea about the Streatham Murder. The only man you can get is a poor devil like Drover.'

'You wanted to talk to me about that, Mr Conder?'

'And the Assistant Commissioner. . . . He may know how to hang a few natives in the jungle, but he's no good for London.'

'I wouldn't say you were wrong about him, Mr Conder. There are a lot of us at the Yard who don't like him. The trouble is he wants to know too much. He won't leave things alone. The Yard's a complicated place. You can't know it all. You can't know all there is about finger-prints if you are going to know all there is about blood tests. He won't understand that. He wants a finger in every pie. F'rinstance, Mr Conder, it would surprise you if you knew where he was

52

tonight. It's his own fault if he gets himself hurt one of these days.'

Conder put down his glass suddenly, and the beer slopped over on to the marble top of the table. 'What's that?' Somebody fell up the stairs. 'For God's sake stop talking shop, Patmore. They are coming up.'

The woman in black velvet frou-froued to the door. 'Quaietly, quaietly, Mr Rowlett,' she breathed to somebody outside. A flushed young man came in. 'Look here, Miss Chick,' he said.

'It's nace to see your face,' Miss Chick said.

'The fellers pushed me from behind. They're all drunk in the bar. Ought to call a policeman.' He stared at Patmore with a glazed eye and then went out again hurriedly. 'You oughtn't to think any harm of him,' Miss Chick said, trailing back to her corner and the beer bottles.

'It's not safe here, Patmore,' Conder said. 'That man Bennett is a suspicious creature. He'd never understand there was no harm in my meeting you.'

'All I want to know, Mr Conder, is what was said about Drover tonight.'

'Why?'

'We want to know what's thought about the case.'

'There you are again. That's Scotland Yard all over. You go on worrying about a man you've got, but you don't know from Adam who cut up Mrs Crowle. I tell you, Patmore, a journalist sees a lot, but that trunk gave me the biggest turn of my life. Old-fashioned, the kind of thing my mother used to take to the sea, and inside thick with blood. Blue stripes like a shirt and thick with blood.'

'I could tell you something about that, Mr Conder. We aren't as slow as you think.'

Conder sipped his beer, his bald gleaming head bent; for a moment he forgot Bennett while he followed a story through the dark streets towards Euston in the wake of a fast car. 'You go and release Ruttledge just because of a few finger-prints.'

'We had no call to keep Ruttledge.'

'You go on worrying about Drover.'

'That's what I want, Mr Conder. Just what did happen tonight about Drover? There were speeches of course, but was anything arranged? Any demonstration? Any propaganda? How did they take it?'

'You are asking a great deal, Patmore,' Conder said. 'You are asking me to betray my friends. Two more Basses, Miss Chick.'

'It's just an exchange of stories, Mr Conder. I'll be able to give you a first-class sensation for your midday edition.'

'You can promise that, exclusive, for certain?'

'Yes, Mr Conder.'

'Well, I'll tell you. Surrogate spoke and Bennett spoke and someone from the garage tried to speak. That's all. Nothing's going to be done about Drover. Everyone'll sign the petition, of course. But you can take it from me, Drover's forgotten. He's as good as taken the drop already. What they are interested in is this fellow at Aldershot who's been given two months for distributing papers. They'll make the hell of a noise about him.'

'Thank you, Mr Conder. That's all I wanted to know.'

'Well, then, drink up your Bass and come away.'

'How are the children, Mr Conder?'

'The children – oh, the children. They're all right. That's to say, one of them has whooping cough.' While Patmore drank his beer, Conder enlarged his tale, the new home, the defective bathroom; every word, every phrase, every fake image was an indictment, an indictment drawn with care to allow no loophole for an acquittal, against life, life without children or wife or home.

'The bill, Miss Chick.'

'Good night, Miss Chick.'

He opened the door; Bennett stood outside.

It was impossible to tell whether he had been listening. He rocked drunkenly on the landing with his hands in his pockets. Conder heard Patmore inside the smoking-room paying a heavy farewell to Miss Chick; he heard Miss Chick say, 'It was nice to see you. We are always very quiet here'; he saw Bennett rocking gently backwards and forwards; he was afraid to go on for fear that Bennett would block the way and afraid to stay for fear of what Patmore might disclose. Then Patmore came out on the landing and said in his heavy cheerful way, 'Sorry to have kept you waiting, Mr Conder. A taking girl that.' Conder stepped forward, Bennett stepped to one side, Patmore went on talking all the way down the stairs. To Conder it seemed that every word was shod with policeman's boots.

'Man there seemed interested,' Patmore said, 'stared at us all the way down. Friend of yours?' Conder had never felt so shaken. On the pavement he stood awhile, after Patmore had left him, and tried to light a cigarette, but the match blew out twice between his fingers. Then he felt threatened by the emptiness of the street and ran for the first lighted corner. A bus roared by, its lights vibrating across the blank glass of an unlit untenanted shop. Scarlet strips of paper read, 'Sale before Lease Expires. Sale before Lease Expires'. He ran a little farther and leant against a shop front. A woman with ravaged restored face said, 'What's the hurry, dear?' and went hopelessly on. 'Sale', ran the notice on the shop. 'Sale. Premises damaged by fire.' It was a pawnbroker's and the window was guarded by iron bars. Watches, old bracelets, a clock and china figures, a shot-gun, the shelves marked the devastation of a hundred homes. He was shaken out of his sense of dissatisfied safety; it seemed to him that the street was falling round him in decay, fires and expiring leases and age pitting the face. He was not himself again until, in a telephone booth across the way, he

55

found the number of his news-editor's house, but with his hand on the receiver, his lips to the black orifice, his heart-beats were normal.

'This is Conder speaking. I'm going to have a lead for the midday. Exclusive. The Ruttledge murder, I think. The Flying Squad went up Euston way. I shouldn't be surprised if there's not a first-class story in it. Yes? Yes? No. Will you put in a paragraph about Drover's petition, keep him alive? They are still interested at the Yard. I don't know why,' but he accepted the news-editor's denial without objection, blown into the ruined street over ten miles of cable: 'The chief's not interested in Drover.'

*

Mr Surrogate leant comfortably back in the taxi and half closed his eyes. He was settled in the past, a past which held no Bennett or Drover, but did not exclude a young woman shaken against him as the hansom jolted over Chelsea Bridge. 'Women's rights,' he said.

'Surely you don't hold the old view – ' and a little later, as the taxi crossed Gower Street, 'Birth Control,' Mr Surrogate said. 'We must have clinics,' and he laid a friendly hand on Kay Rimmer's knee. A street lamp shot a ray of light into the dark interior, and Mr Surrogate, catching a glimpse of her smiling expectation, withdrew his hand suddenly. One mustn't be rash; it was so easy to be misunderstood; and he trod very softly ahead of her up the stairs to the first floor of the converted house, afraid that the landlord might appear out of his sitting-room by the entrance. He was glad that Davis slept out.

'I live all alone here,' Mr Surrogate said, a little stiffly and sadly, 'my wife is dead.' He switched on a light and the white walls rose round him. 'Have a nut while I light the fire?' He knelt and the gentle hissing flames sprang from his match-end.

56

'It's lovely here,' Kay Rimmer said. 'What a lot of books you have.'

'Those are my own,' Mr Surrogate said.

'It must be wonderful to write.'

'One tries to exert an influence. Would you like to see the flat? It's small, but choice, I think. Of course,' Mr Surrogate added with lowered respectful voice, 'it lacks the female touch. A man's den.' But the word den was a shocking misnomer; Mr Surrogate went from room to room switching on the lights, and everywhere he went white panelling, cream walls, pale jade walls sprang, like sentries, to attention. He never looked round; he was aware behind him of her dumb approval. No woman's taste could have been more adequate; the few objects which broke the bareness of the drawing-room and dining-room were chosen with an impeccable appreciation: a papier-mâché tea-caddy, a glass painting, a slender painted Empire table in the jade room. Mr Surrogate padded ahead, switching on the lights; he drew attention to nothing; with his smooth blond head deprecatingly bent he might have been the humble custodian of his treasures; no one could have guessed the fierce smothered pride which bowed his head in recognition of his own perfect taste.

'My bedroom,' he said a little drily, opening a pink door, turning on several lights. Kay Rimmer gave a gasp of pleasure at the rose hangings, the semi-circular bed, the silk bedspread like a waste of fallen petals.

'Oh,' she said, catching sight of the great mirror with its deep reflections, which flattered her more than a soft-spoken man. 'Oh,' she said again at sight of the only picture on the walls, 'how lovely. Who's that?'

Mr Surrogate answered without looking: 'My wife.' It faced the bed. It was the first face he saw in the morning. It greeted him, before Davis, with its beauty and its malice and its integrity.

'How you must have loved her,' Kay Rimmer said softly, under the spell of the face, and for a moment Mr Surrogate longed to tell the truth, that it was hung there as an atonement for his dislike, as a satisfaction for his humility, because of its reminder of the one woman who had never failed to see through him. 'Let me show you the kitchen,' he said quickly.

The kitchen was like a snowdrift with its white casement and white dresser and white table and enamelled gas stove and its deep blue walls and ceiling. The lights in the back rooms of the houses opposite glinted on the walls; a car complained in the mews between. 'You can see what everyone's doing,' Kay Rimmer said, standing at the window. Through the chink of the curtains on a top floor she saw a woman brushing her hair; a great double bed waited for its inhabitants; a maid laid breakfast; a man wrote letters; a chauffeur lent from the window of a little flat above a garage and smoked his last pipe.

'Everyone doing something different,' she said, her eyes going back to the double bed and her thoughts on the pink bedspread in the other room and Jules and half a loaf is better than no bread and the lovely dead indifferent woman on the wall. Her body was ready for enjoyment; the deep peace of sensuality covered all the fears and perplexities of the day; she never felt more at home than in a bed or a man's arms.

*

Conrad Drover, attaché case in hand, walked all the way to Battersea. He could not bring himself to spend any pence on bus or tube that might be spent on his brother's petition. His brother was the only man he loved in the world, and his brother for the first time in his life needed him; strength for the first time needed brains. Before it had always been brains which had needed strength, cleverness which had needed stupidity. All the way down Oakley Street and along the Embankment a child ran scurrying to the corner of the playground where his brother beat a ball against the wall; the trams came screeching like a finger drawn on glass up the curve of Battersea Bridge and down into the ill-lighted network of streets beyond; on the water the gulls floated asleep. Into the darkness of the secondary school Conrad fell, alone without his brother, his name tossed across the asphalt – 'He's called Conrad, Conrad, Conrad.' His brother sat in a steel cage driving through the rain; he earned three pounds a week; Conrad sat at a desk aware of the hatred behind him, in the school, in the office; the cold recognition of his efficiency through the glass door of the headmaster's room, of the manager's room; Conrad earned six pounds a week.

The cold railings round the Battersea Polytechnic touched the backs of his hands; Conrad Drover walked on towards the woman he loved more than any other woman. He opened the letter from his brother at his desk and read with despair, 'married on Tuesday'; it was weeks before he realized that Milly had not robbed him of his brother's stupidity and serenity and strength.

A notice on the railings said: 'It is forbidden to throw stones at the Polytechnic.'

There was nothing that either of them had ever been able to do for his brother; they had come together in their admiration and impotence, sitting as it were in his shadow away from the world which rocked and roared around them. Now he was gone and it was they who had to have strength. All day in Court Conrad had prayed that he might be lent stupidity, so that he might not recognize what lay behind the three white wigs, the silk robes, the whispers, the getting up and the sitting down: 'I submit, m'lud, that if you look at Rex v. Hindle'; the coughing and the complete lack of interest. A child ran into him chasing a ball, and Conrad clutched a railing for support. He thought with bitterness of Kay: 'The manager would sack me. You are different. You have brains.' If ever I have a child, he thought, I shall pray that he will be born stupid.

The oldest judge put his head on his hand and said wearily: 'We have given counsel for the defence the greatest possible latitude. He has taken up a great deal of time with irrelevancies.' He seemed surprised and a little shocked at the ingenuity of the attempt to save the accused man. Ingenuity but not passion; the two counsel nodded and becked and exchanged compliments; once they became a little acrid over Rex v. Hindle; but afterwards in the corridor Conrad Drover saw them arm in arm going off to lunch. 'Of course I hadn't a chance.' 'You did splendidly. I could see the solicitors were impressed.' And afterwards in Piccadilly, on the steps of the Berkeley, he had heard the thin man with a jaundiced face say: 'A pram on top of a taxi,' and laugh. Conrad Drover had recognized him. On the same day as his brother's fate was decided, the Assistant Commissioner could laugh at a stupid joke. His brother was just one of many men strung up for justice. The old judge said in a kind voice: 'Counsel for the defence has argued with great skill on the question of motive. He has tried to show that the jury were improperly directed. . . .' A young barrister just behind Conrad said: 'I'm off to old Symond's Court. There's nothing more of interest here. See you in hall.' When the door opened Conrad could hear someone sweeping in the long passage outside. The old judge said: 'We have come to the conclusion that no cause has been shown for setting aside the decision of the jury.'

His brother lived in a basement flat opposite the laurels and the railings of the Polytechnic. Conrad looked down and saw beneath his feet the yellow glow of the kitchen. The tenement disappeared unlit into the sky. It was like a monument above a tomb, and a light showed that someone was awake in the tomb. He rang the bell and waited. Everything was as usual, even to the footsteps and the glimmer of light which went on behind the door, even to his following Milly in silence down the stone stairs to the kitchen. They had never had much to say to each other, but it was true, he thought, as she opened the door and led him into the glow of gas among the clean stacked plates, that this was the first time they had been completely alone. One did not need to be alone with Milly to love her more than any other woman. She was not beautiful. She was small and fair and thin, her hands were too large, and she had high prominent cheekbones in a face which was too generous to be beautiful. Some women were like audited account books, the proportion of every part was entered in double column and checked and found correct, but Milly's accounts were of a bankrupt firm, they did not balance; but this failure to balance had an extravagant generosity.

In the kitchen they kissed with quick formality, as if it were a courtesy to be got through before the important business. He looked at the table, at the stove. 'You've had no supper.'

She said: 'I'm not hungry,' and then lied, 'I had a big tea.' The lie was not meant to deceive. It was a warning, which he understood, that everything must be said and acted on the usual plane. She was dug in so inefficiently against emotion that she was afraid of almost anything he might do. He said: 'I'm going to fry some bacon,' and she did not dare to make any protest. While the bacon sizzled in the pan he began to talk very fast, so fast that soon the words were almost unintelligible. 'We had an interesting case yesterday. Suspected arson. The man set fire to part of his shop, so we think. We were going to contest his claim, but he dropped it quite suddenly, and we're leaving it at that. He put the fire out himself, so it never came to the police. Name of Bernay. Just one room, a lot of stuff burned, and a lot more spoilt. Now why did he drop the claim? Afraid we'd be able to prove arson? The manager doesn't believe it. He believes he didn't care a damn about the claim, he wanted to get rid of the stuff, perhaps it was stolen and the police were watching and he got the wind up, not our business anyway.' He looked up suddenly with horror, watching her from the other side of the stove across the thin smoke from the spitting fat. As clearly as if she had spoken he was aware of her thoughts clinging round the words fire, police, burned. 'No,' he said, 'No. You must take care of yourself. There's still hope.' The words were bundles of grenades flung into her parapet.

'You don't believe it.' He watched with pain and tenderness her white hopeless face, her shoulders a little bent with the weight of five happy years. He became aware with sudden clarity how injustice did not belong only to an old tired judge, to a policeman joking in Piccadilly; it was as much a part of the body as age and inevitable disease. There was no such thing as justice in the air we breathed, for it was those who hated and envied and married for money or convenience who were happy. Death could not hurt them, it could only hurt those who loved. Intolerable the weight of those happy years, of days in the Park and nights at the pictures, of the shared bed and the shared meal and the shared misery.

She said: 'I shouldn't mind if he was dying here. I could look after him. We'd be together all day and all night.' She convinced herself of how happy she could be with him dying upstairs, her eyes shone for a moment with the false happiness of her day-dream, that he was dying in the room upstairs. His love of his brother wavered at the sight of her despair. 'Why did he do it?' he protested.

'The policeman was going to hit me,' she said. 'Everyone was excited.' She began to shake all over as if she were again in the centre of the mob near Hyde Park Corner. They straddled across Rotten Row, kicking up the dust into thin smoke, and the riders turned their gleaming groomed mounts and trotted hurriedly back while the crowd shouted and laughed at them. An unemployed man waved a banner by the Achilles statue.

'I saw Kay. She was off to a party meeting. They'll have to do something for him.'

The crowd turned and ran as the mounted police came down the Row with drawn staves. The man by the Achilles statue struck out with his banner at two policemen who pulled him to the ground and twisted his arms behind his back. He shouted for help, but the crowd was fighting to get away from the wedge of police who were driving them towards the gates. The great green plains of the Park were dotted with shabby men running away.

'They won't do anything for him,' Milly said, flinching again at the raised truncheon and the fear of a pain which never came. The policeman was on his knees bleeding into the turf and crying and gasping, and the crowd was suddenly very far away and the three of them were alone with the grass and a park chair and a sense of disaster. The policeman's face was wet with tears.

'You've got to have some supper. Look, the bacon's ready.'

'I'm not hungry.' Conrad pulled out a chair and made her sit down. He took a warm plate from the oven and laid the bacon on it. He was almost happy, making her eat.

'Can't you do something, Conrad? You're clever.' The words from her were not an insult as they had been from Kay.

'I'm going to look after you till he's back. You must have a man in the house.'

'There isn't a room.'

'I'll make up a bed on the floor here.'

'All right. But I don't need anyone. I don't need anything.' But she contradicted herself a moment later. 'Isn't there anything I can do? Think of something I can do.' He drew a chair to the table beside her and sat down. 'I'll think of something. Don't be afraid.' But he himself, with his head in his hands, pretending to think, was dizzy with fear. She was appealing to him. He was being asked for help, and the only help he had been trained to give was adding and subtracting, multiplying and dividing. The whole office depended on him, directors driving up in their cars, nodding presently over the green baize in the board room, shareholders leaping to their feet and asking petulantly what this figure meant, why that figure was not accounted for; but the dependence of one individual left him dizzy with fear.

'I'm afraid without him here,' she said. Jim had sat for the last five years in one chair in one place in the kitchen and they had talked and laughed and had hardly noticed how their nerves and their cleverness had been quietened by his serene obtuseness. 'Tell me what to do. He always said you had the brains.'

Conrad stared at the spread newspapers on the kitchen table. His mnd took the opportunity to shirk its task, wandering across the columns of type, picking up a headline here and a headline there: 'Mr MacDonald to fly home to Lossiemouth'; 'Are you Insured?', 'Spot the Stars'.

'We ought to use influence. Everything goes by influence,' he said, thinking of the brothers on the board, the nephew in the clerks' room. But he was daunted the next moment by his own and Milly's insignificance. He heard the world humming with the voices of generals and politicians, bishops and surgeons and schoolmasters, who knew what they wanted, who knew what everyone else wanted: 'I have a cousin, an uncle, a nephew, a niece,' the world humming and vibrating with the pulling of wires. Milly's face was lost among the harsh confident cultured faces. It did not belong to the same world; they were insulated against pain, poverty and dis-aster. One could not appeal to them for justice; justice to them was another word for prison.

'But how?'

'Spot the Stars', he read. 'Are you Insured? Mr MacDo-nald – ' There was a photograph of the Prince of Wales opening a new hostel for the unemployed; he was sur-rounded by men in frock coats carrying top hats; women in fur coats pressed round the edge of the picture gazing at the golden key. An officer and his bride stepped out of St Mar-garet's into the blaze of publicity under arched swords. A shabby woman with a cameo brooch seemed out of place on the same page: 'Mrs Coney, wife of the murdered police constable.'

'Have you seen this?'

The photograph roused her for a moment from the dull-ness of her despair. Her happiness had always been shot through with touches of malice. Her husband contented with his job and his pay had been the Communist; not Milly, contented with nothing but his love, suspicious of the whole world outside. She had never believed that they would be left alone to enjoy each other. Her malice had been a form of defence, an appeal to other people to 'leave us alone'. She said now, looking at the photograph, in the usual tone of exaggerated dislike: 'She reminds me of – She looks like – ' but she had been robbed of her only weapon; the woman reminded her of nothing, staring bleakly out, an in-imical stranger, into the warm clean kitchen, but of the policeman on his knees crying with pain and fear in the Park.

'Go and see her,' Conrad said. 'If she'd sign the petition the news would be in every newspaper. Something would be done.' The photograph seemed no longer out of place on that page of celebrities; Mrs Coney too had influence.

'She'd never do it.'

'Go and try tomorrow. I know it'll be difficult to go and beg – '

'It'll be easy,' Milly said. 'I wasn't thinking of that. I was thinking what I'd do. If Jim had been killed and that woman (Coney, indeed, she's like a starved rat) came and asked me to help her husband.' Conrad watched her with satisfaction; he had given her something to do and she no longer despaired; she was malicious and herself again. 'Go on,' he said, 'what would you do?'

'I'd want to pull her hair and scratch her face,' Milly said, 'but I suppose really – I suppose I'd sign the petition. What's done can't be undone, can it?' But the saying, spoken on innumerable occasions, over spilt milk, over broken glass, over burnt pastry, played her false. It lay like a high wall between five happy years and the present. You had to remember what was on the other side. You had to strain your mind to recall the details of uneventful evenings. They could not be repeated. 'Think of something else we can do. Think. Think.'

Conrad thought. But the only thought which would come was of his last meeting with his brother, in a place the size of a telephone box, where you couldn't speak and look at the same time. A look through the glass. A word through the wire. Conrad said, with his hand spread over Mrs Coney's features: 'We've got to consider something else.' His brother had asked him, 'How's Milly? Keep an eye on Milly.' It was his duty therefore to let her see the worst. There was something he was sure Milly had not considered; to have considered it did not belong to her quietness, her generosity and her malice; it belonged to his own cleverness, the cleverness of addition and subtraction, of balancing books, of double entries. 'We've got to remember that if he gets his reprieve he may be in prison for eighteen years. He's thirty-eight now. He'd be fifty-six when he came out, and you would be forty-five.'

She took him by surprise. 'I've thought of that. Of course I've thought of that. But what's the good of thinking? He'd rather be alive than dead. I'll go and see her tomorrow.' But the long silence after her protest showed that she had not thought of it. The idea came to her suddenly and plainly of what she might lose; she felt it like a withering of the skin, the death of her sex. When he came out of prison, she would be without passion or enjoyment. 'You can't divorce a man in prison,' Conrad said. He was afraid of her anger, but she was only astonished. 'I wouldn't divorce him. We love each other.'

'Of course,' he said. 'I can understand that. I love him too. More than anyone. I love him more than I love you.'

'You've no cause to love me.' He wanted to tell her that he had the same reason as his brother had; he wanted to describe her to herself, the fair fine hair, the high cheekbones, the large mouth and the large hands and the small body; the courage of her malice and the fidelity of her despair. 'You've no cause to,' she said again. 'We've laughed at you. Kay and I have. How often,' she said with a long sigh for the happy malicious past, 'I've called you an old woman. Your white face and your twitchings. And now,' she went on, smiling unwillingly, 'you are better than a house without a man in it. When you've been married five years it seems odd to be alone in a house with a girl. And of course,' she said with generosity, 'you've got the brains.'

'Kay doesn't think much of them.'

'Oh, you needn't mind what Kay thinks. There's only one thing Kay wants in a man and that's not brains.'

'I'll come tomorrow night,' Conrad said. She got up from the table and came and sat on its edge close to him. 'You ought to go home to bed now,' she said. 'You look tired to death. You've been working too hard. It was good of you to come. I feel happier a lot with that idea for tomorrow. I don't see how she can say no.'

'You oughtn't to expect too much.'

Milly said with an impatient flash of anger: 'You don't expect enough. There you are, always looking as if you'd got the sack, and you're chief clerk and you've got six pounds a week. Why don't you say to yourself every day, "I'm a success. I'm a success"? If I had you here for a month, we'd see something different.'

'Yes. What? Tell me?' He sat back with a foolish uneasy smile at the thought of her company.

'I'd give you lots of porridge. I'd make you sleep a lot. Your nerves are all wrong. Hold out your hand. Look how it wobbles. You wouldn't be much good with a gun. Oh, if I had you here a month, I'd make a man of you. You're better already. Look at you smiling. You're different.'

'You aren't the same. I've never heard you talk as much as this.'

'I've never needed to talk before,' she said. Exhilaration and forgetfulness wavered in her face like a paper scrap in a high wind; tossed on the currents of air it floated a moment and then was blown to earth in the gusts of misery. 'I've got nothing to do but talk, talk.'

'Your nerves are as bad as mine.' He caught her hands and said: 'Help me and I'll help you. Talk to me as you did just now, and I'll, I'll – '

'What can you do? There's nothing anyone can do. That woman won't be able to do anything. No one. They've got him and they'll keep him. No one likes people to be happy. If we hadn't been so happy, he wouldn't be there. He wouldn't have stabbed that man. We'd be together. I never wanted to be happy. I was always afraid.'

'I'll think of something,' Conrad said.

*

She thought of his promise with gratitude but without much hope as she went up the stone stairs to the bedroom on the ground floor. The whole house, even the unknown floors above, seemed draughty with emptiness. She had been the only tenant for the last six weeks, since the old woman with a beard had gone off hurriedly in a two-seater car driven by a young man – a bedstead, two chairs and a dressing-table piled in the dicky and on the lowered hood. A day later the bailiffs had come, and heavy pieces of furniture had been lowered stair by stair, shaking her bedroom walls, flaking the plaster from the basement ceiling.

Milly took off her dress, put on her dressing-gown and began to brush her hair. Outside, the front door creaked in the wind and the draught stirred the mat. Anybody could get in, for the lock of the door was broken, and she wondered why she had not asked Conrad to stay. Again she was astonished at the change, that she should depend on Conrad. He had never, while Jim was there, been quite real to her, he had only been a quality Jim lacked, the quality of brain, the quality of nerves. Now he was a man in the house, a fellow drop of human life to make the vast emptiness of the house seem less complete.

Many nights when Kay was out and Jim on night duty she had been alone for hours with lifting mats and creaking doors, but she had not cared, lying in bed with her eyes open in the dark, keeping her happiness all the time in mind because she knew it would not go on for ever. And the thermos of hot tea and the plate of sandwiches in the kitchen had been all the company she needed.

A board squeaked above her head and the mat lifted. She thought: Kay will be home soon. What has she been doing all this while? Are they helping Jim? But she did not believe it, her mind dwelling again on the green spaces of the Park and the men running away. She turned from the mirror to the empty bed, but she did not go to it. She eyed it with sad repulsion, the white turned-down sheet, the two pillows. She hardly recognized it. It was as empty as the house, as cold as the draught under doors. He ought to be lying in it, tired out with the day's driving, but waking when she joined him. She had always felt safe in bed beside him, feeling the shape of his bones like the roughness of a wall. Now the bed was the map of a strange continent, a blank space waiting to be explored through many years, and she thought again with a sense of stupefaction: 'If they let him off, I shall be forty-five.' The emptiness of the floors above pressed on her again like the emptiness of years. 'He'd rather be alive than dead,' she thought, but she could not feel sure. She had always known what he wanted; when they were together, when they were in different rooms, when she was at home and he was at the garage, the thoughts of his slow brain had always flashed vividly in hers. But now, because she could not imagine his surroundings, could not tell whether he was awake or asleep, communication was barred. Although they loved each other, their minds were like two countries at war, with the telegraph wires down and the rails torn up.

The door creaked again. Sitting on the edge of her bed, she wished Kay would come home. The thought of the empty floors above her head was becoming difficult to bear. Dust and broken sashes and the mice running behind the skirting board. She had felt happier even when the strange old woman with a beard was living up there. She, too, must have been miserable, afraid of the bailiffs, planning secretly her evasion with the bedstead, two chairs and a dressing-table, and a year ago, before Milly had felt the need to fill vacant spaces with human life, a mother and six children had lived in the two rooms at the top of the house. Now she would have welcomed the crying in the night, the noises on the stairs, the constant turbulent activity, like a pudding on the boil.

She said aloud: 'I can't stand it,' and made suddenly for the door. It was as if her own footprints in the dust on the boards would make the rooms less empty, as if she could

70

people them with scraps and cast-offs of her unhappiness. The electric lights had been turned off on the stairs and the bulbs had been stolen. She felt her way stair by stair, while her skin stiffened with the cold. When a board creaked she was not afraid. It would have been easy for a tramp to spend the night on the unused stairs, but even if she had put her hand on a face, she would not have started. She could not have said what gave her courage; whether it was because there was nothing in death for her now to shrink from or whether the thought of murder no longer terrified her because her husband was a murderer. But the stairs were as empty as the rooms through which she walked. The moonlight through the unprotected glass made them into blue cold shabby squares like the used ice at a fishmongers'. In one room she found in the grate a ball of hair combings as large as a baby's skull and on the floor in another room an unreceipted bill for a pair of corsets. She made her way to the top, to the two rooms where there was only a smell of stale air and a dead bat on the floor, like a bundle of brown knitting. It must have come down the chimney and never found its way out again.

A door opened and shut below and Milly trailed her dressing-gown down the bare stairs. On the first floor landing a whiff of scent blew up to her and in the light from her bedroom she saw Kay pulling off her gloves. Milly felt shy before her younger sister. She stood at the edge of loneliness, carrying a little of the vacancy of empty rooms in her blue abashed eyes, while Kay brought in with her a world of men. After five years of marriage Milly felt inexperienced and stupidly innocent in front of Kay.

'What on earth, Milly? What are you doing up there?'

'I couldn't sleep. Have you been to the meeting?'

'Yes.'

'Are they going to do anything?'

'Everyone's signed the petition.' Milly came down the

stairs and went into her room and sat down on her bed. 'But, Milly,' Kay called from her own room on the other side of the passage, 'that's not all. Mr Surrogate's going to do something. He's going to use influence. A lady he knows.'

Milly took off her dressing-gown, turned off the light and got into bed. The light from Kay's room shone across the passage and into her own room. 'I went home with him,' Kay said. 'Such a lovely flat he's got. His wife's dead, and there's a beautiful picture of her. I thought he was going to make love to me, but he didn't. He just talked. Marriage and Birth Control. It was like a rubber shop. I'm going to meet him again tomorrow night, and then we'll see the sparks fly.'

The door creaked and the mat lifted and Kay talked. The wind prowled round Battersea and laid a damp mark on the window pane. 'It was raining and he sent me all the way home in a taxi.' Milly thought: I shall be forty-five, and in the puzzled despair of the idea for a moment fell asleep. 'Tomorrow night,' Kay said, brushing her hair one hundred times. Milly dreamed, with a shiver of fear and pleasure, that Jim was covering her with his body, and presently they were still and happy and deeply contented. But she woke again almost immediately to the thought of Conrad's shaking hand. A woman might as well marry a leaf, she thought with proud malice because Jim was as firm as a wall and even his stupidity had strength. But then she remembered the Park, the prison, the judge, and was angry with his stupidity and strength. She remembered the empty rooms, the bundle of hair combings, the unpaid bill and the dead bat. What was the good of loving me if you do this to me?

Kay said: 'He has the loveliest pink bedroom.' She sat with her forehead almost touching the glass, hearing, as she did every night, the pounding of the machines, the rattle of the falling boxes.

*

'Drop me here,' the Assistant Commissioner said at the corner of Great College Street, and he stiffened in an elderly irritated way as the secretary's hand fell on his knee. 'You won't forget,' the secretary said, 'old Beale depends on you.' Since leaving the prison he had become increasingly intimate; it was the measure of his intimacy that he now spoke of 'old Beale' and not of 'the Minister'. The Assistant Commissioner wondered, with a complete lack of self-confidence, what he would do if the young man addressed him too by name, without the prefix of his rank. He was not used to these sudden intimacies; his background was filled with nephews and subalterns who called him 'sir'. He said as quickly as he could: 'Of course. I don't – er – forget things,' and fled up the street. He had never felt so ill at ease and it took all the length of the old Westminster street, with its sparse lighting and worn respectable fronts, its atmosphere of dowagers' drawing-rooms, to restore his nerve. Behind the tall upper windows old ladies in silks spoke softly of meeting Mr Browning in Florence to old men with white moustaches, whose interest in racing had never survived the ecstatic moment of Persimmon's passing. Twenty feet below them stepped the neat elderly figure with the yellow face, his thoughts turned on Flossie Matthews raped on Streatham Common.

The light in his flat showed that Mrs Simpson was waiting in for him. He had ordered a light supper at six, so that he might work uninterrupted on the Streatham and Paddington reports. The Assistant Commissioner before he entered the doorway glanced over his shoulder. The movement was pure habit; in the East it was necessary always to watch the road behind; it was a condition of survival. He opened the door of his flat and the pale blond face of the secretary fled from his mind; he was surrounded by the comforting accumulated rubbish of his life, the native weapons, the pipe racks, the decorated gourds, the carved tobacco jars, Mrs Simpson

73

with her twisted bun of grey hair and her vexed fidelity. Her small lined face was the size of a head-hunter's shrivelled skull. She began to complain before he had shut the door: 'Half an hour late. I thought you were never comin' in. You asked for early supper.'

He never troubled to answer Mrs Simpson. They understood one another. She liked to talk and he liked to be silent.

'Your supper's spoilt anyway.'

He walked past her into the dining-room and saw at once the writing on the telephone memorandum. 'Please ring Superintendent Crosse.'

'He rang up twenty minutes ago. He said he'd tried to get you at the hotel, but you'd gone. I said I didn't know where you'd been gallivantin'.'

'Central 2375.'

'More than my place is worth to complain, I said. I said he'd ordered his supper early, an' now it'll be spoilt.'

'Is that you, Crosse?'

Mrs Simpson went out and slammed the door.

For some time the Assistant Commissioner listened in silence to the gruff suspicious voice which told him that the murderer of Mrs Janet Crowle was known. He heard of the small, terribly discreet tobacconist who had dropped into the Yard at five-thirty 'all of a tremble'. It was extraordinary how often a case presented a blank wall up to the last moment, and then the rush of information became almost embarrassing. The tobacconist was still being examined by Crosse when the laundry rang up, and ten minutes later a frightened landlady told her story to the Euston police.

'You are going to pull him in tonight?'

'Yes, she says he'll be in all the evening. He has a service revolver.'

'What are your arrangements?'

'I've got two men watching the house. I don't want any

trouble with firearms. The landlady's going to let us in quietly and we'll nab him before he gets to his gun. We're leaving in half an hour.'

The Assistant Commissioner looked at his watch. 'I'll be with you in twenty minutes.'

'It's quite unnecessary, sir,' the voice said more suspiciously than ever.

'It's all right. You'll take control. I only want to see how things are done over here. One must – er – know the ropes. What's that you said?'

'Nothing, sir.'

'Oh, and Crosse. Will you see to this at once? About Drover. The Minister wants to gauge the effect of a reprieve. Get the stations to make inquiries. Quietly. Send in confidential reports. They – er – won't be held, held responsible for mistakes. You might get something out of the Press. Do what you can. I leave it to you, but let me have the – er – reports. Get to it at once. We've only got a few days.'

The Assistant Commissioner rang off. He knew quite well what Crosse was saying now, his complaints and criticisms travelling down the narrow corridors, in and out of the little glass waiting-rooms. 'Have you heard the latest? Do you know what he's up to now? Interfering. Finger in every pie. Can't leave a man to his job.' He had turned too quickly from the telephone and for a moment he held to the edge of the table, with his head a little bent. Any quick movement made him dizzy. There was nothing wrong with him except age. After fifty-six years the world was likely to make any man dizzy.

Soon the gourds and the tobacco racks and the native weapons steadied, but the Assistant Commissioner felt curiously unwilling to leave his flat and return to the Yard. 'Interfering. Fingers in every pie.' Six months of continuous criticism and obstruction were wearing his nerves thin. In the

East he had always interfered; he had been expected to inter-
fere; they had needed his advice. The three-year spells of
duty allowed no one to dig himself in, but the little glass
rooms along the passages at Scotland Yard were like the
deep dugouts of an intricate trench system. He couldn't ask a
question without troubling some inspector's self-import-
ance. They could not understand his motives. He was not
threatening them; he had not been appointed to 'clean
up' the Yard; he had been appointed to a job and he only
wanted to learn his job. He opened the door of the dining-
room and said a little wearily to Mrs Simpson in the kitchen: 'I shall not want, not, not, that's to say I'm – er –
going out.'

'An' what about this supper? Here I've been slavin' away,
out of hours, when I'm wanted at home, and all the thanks I
get – '

'Eat it yourself, Mrs Simpson.'

She emerged from the kitchen, small, grey and furious,
wiping her hands on her apron. Behind her was a wavering
of steam and a smell of burning food. Mrs Simpson was not
a good cook, but the Assistant Commissioner did not notice
his food. He ate, turned sideways, with his eyes on a newspaper or a report; when he occasionally remarked that he
had had a good dinner, he meant that the report or the newspaper had pleased him.

'Good night, Mrs Simpson.' But her fury and her fidelity
held him with his hand on the door; he could not turn his
back before allowing her her 'say'. She was old and withered, angry and unreasonable, but he recognized a quality he
shared; it might be described loosely as love, as obstinacy, as
loneliness, or even as desperation. The more one was alone,
the more one clung to one's job, the only thing it was certainly right to do, the only human value valid for every
change of government, and for every change of heart. 'It's
them murderers,' Mrs Simpson said with hatred. 'I'd like to

76

see 'em all strung up and finished with. That Drover.' She quivered in the steam under the weight of the years, and death lent her hatred and contempt its own blindness and incongruity. 'Good food wasted.'

At the Yard he found that his directions had already been carried out. They were careful never to give him reason for legitimate complaints; they sprang to his orders as they would never have sprung to the orders of a man they liked. Then there would have been a certain give and take, an occasional pardonable slackness, but with him they were careful that the only grounds of complaint should be theirs for his intrusion. The stations had already been informed of his instructions regarding Drover. They had even kept the tobacconist at the Yard in case the Assistant Commissioner wished to see him, and a careful report on the developments in the Paddington murder lay already on his desk. He tried in vain to break through their politeness and disapproval. 'I'm not troubling to read this, Crosse. It's your job. I'm your, your – er – subordinate tonight. I merely want to – want to learn.' Superintendent Crosse's face was as blank as a whitewashed wall.

They packed into a single car. The great lit globe of the Coliseum balanced above the restaurants and the cafés and the public-houses in St Martin's Lane. Round and round Trafalgar Square the buses went like circus horses. The high squeal of the Wolseley's hooter pierced through a traffic block; cars ground their brakes, a policeman raised his hand, and they were shaken out into Charing Cross Road temporarily bare of traffic. The whores flowed down one pavement and up another; flat dago faces printed on song sheets filled the window of a music shop and a salesman inside played with passionate melancholy: 'My Baby Don't Care'. A row of men peered into peepshows, and 'A Night in Paris' and 'What the Butler Saw' and 'For Women Only' rattled and whined and jolted and stuck. Somebody was firing a rifle in a fun booth for cigarette packets and china vases.

'Have you brought a gun, sir?' Crosse asked.

'I don't possess one,' the Assistant Commissioner said.

A gust of wind and rain brushed the windows in St Giles's Circus and lifted the posters of a man selling papers by Lyons Corner House, so that for a moment, while a bus delayed them, the Assistant Commissioner caught a résumé of the evening's news, poster after poster flapping up: 'Home to Lossiemouth', '3.30 Results', 'Insured?' 'Appeal Fails', 'Midday Runners'; then falling again, like time burying the old news deep.

'You ought to have brought a gun, sir.'

The car dived left by Goodge Street Station, and then right, up Charlotte Street.

'I've never felt the need of one yet.'

The Superintendent swallowed. He wanted to say something disparaging, something which would put the East and its jungles in a proper place in the hierarchy of danger. 'He's got a gun, sir.'

'He'll be afraid to use it,' the Assistant Commissioner said. He had walked for twenty miles through the jungle with a walking-stick and he wasn't going to carry a revolver within two miles of Scotland Yard. He did not believe that the man who had killed Mrs Janet Crowle and later cut up the body and stowed it in a trunk in the left luggage department at Paddington was a braver man than the murderer who had set fire to his own hut and died in the flames to escape capture. If one could go out against men like that with a walking stick, one did not need a weapon in London.

The car came out for a moment into the Euston Road, sent its shrill warning past the furniture dealers' and wireless shops and one-night hotels to the constable on point duty, then swerved across the lit garish road into the darkness again. A man stepped out from a tobacconist's and waved to them, and the car slid to the kerb and stopped. Behind them Euston Road flickered and grumbled, but in the street no one spoke, no one moved except the man who fumbled at the door of the car. Crosse helped him from inside and leaning across asked softly: 'Well?'

'He's going out,' the man said. 'He's asked the landlady for hot water and a clean towel. She told him she'd have to boil a kettle and slipped downstairs and told Jenks.'

'We'd better get him in the house,' Crosse said. 'Which is it?'

'You'll see Jenks in the doorway fifty yards down on the left-hand side.'

'Which is the room?'

'Top floor. Back room. There's a fire escape up the back outside the window. He hasn't drawn the curtains, the landlady says. He never draws 'em before supper. He's a man of habits.'

'Does he face the window?'

'His armchair faces the door.'

'Has he had the hot water?'

'Jenks'll signal when she takes it up,' and while he spoke a tiny flame shone in the street and went out. 'There,' the man said. 'She's taking up the water now.'

'Come on,' Crosse said, 'out of the car. Two men stand in the doorway where Jenks is, one round to the back door, one up the fire escape. I'll go up the stairs with Jenks. How do you reach the fire escape?'

'A passage on the right of the front door,' the man said, 'takes you to the back yard. You can't help seeing the fire escape.'

'I'll go up the fire escape,' the Assistant Commissioner said.

'You'd better stay in the street,' Crosse said. 'But I haven't got the time to argue now. Come on quietly.' They

79

crossed the road and followed him down the pavement, a line of heavy men in soft hats walking cumbrously on tiptoe; only the Assistant Commissioner at the tail of the procession walked with natural lightness, all the useless flesh burned away by fever. A taxi went soberly by towards Euston and a young man in horn-rimmed glasses leant out of the window and stared at them with his mouth open. 'Hi!' he said in a tipsy voice, 'Hi!'; they walked on self-consciously like a row of ducks, while the taxi receded and the young man still leant from the window and called: 'Hi!' drunk and puzzled and amused; as the taxi turned into Euston Road he hammered on the glass and called to the driver to look: 'Lot of funny men,' they heard him shout. Lights behind upper windows shrouded in lace curtains never touched the dark channel in which they walked. They were buried twenty feet deep in a night world of their own; above their heads the lights behind closed panes, at their backs a gleam and murmur, the faint evocation of a world in uproar till the midnight closing hour. Somebody whispered from a doorway: 'He's washing now.'

Crosse halted them and whispered back: 'How long have we got?'

'He always washes well when he goes out of an evening, the landlady says. Down to the waist. She says he's always been a one for cleanliness.'

The Assistant Commissioner smiled, treading softly down a brick-paved passage to the back door. (Behind him he could hear Crosse put up his safety catch.) With his hands on the iron rail of the fire escape, he thought of innumerable clerics rising in innumerable pulpits to talk of cleanliness as next to godliness (the rails struck cold through his gloves, and it was difficult to mount quietly, the nails on his shoes striking the steel steps), praising the clean body as an indication of the clean mind. He thought of Crippen shaving carefully every day of his trial, particular about small things.

It was these contradictions, the moral maxims which did not apply, that made it impossible for a man to found his life on any higher motive than doing his job. A life spent with criminals would never fail to strip the maxims of priests and teachers from the underlying chaos.

The moon burnt for a moment through the clouded sky and silvered the rails and the steps of the fire escape, showed the huddle of chimney pots above him, and dimmed the light in the top room. It travelled between the clouds with the swiftness of a car, and the whole globe heeled over with it. The Assistant Commissioner clutched the rail and lowered his head, attacked again by dizziness. Every attack was followed by a great fear, not the fear of death, but the fear of enforced retirement, a fear which he fought with his efficiency, his hesitations which conserved his energy, and his meticulousness. With that chill at his brain he mounted the last steps.

A man was talking. He could hear the voice before he could see the face. The window above was open.

'Come to Jesus,' the voice said. 'Come to Jesus.' The Assistant Commissioner mounted slowly; there was no lamp in the yard below, there was darkness everywhere now that the moon had gone, except where the bulb in the room lit a few feet of steel platform and a step or two. 'Oh, come to Jesus all of you. Come to Jesus.' The Assistant Commissioner was alone with the voice. The policeman at the back door, in the pool of night, made no sound; the house had swallowed up Crosse and his companions. 'Don't think I don't understand you. Oh, I've sinned too, friends, believe me, I've sinned too.' The Assistant Commissioner's shoe struck a spark on the penultimate step, but the voice with its absurd unction and its intolerable theatricality went on. 'I've got a bleeding heart, friends. If you could see inside – '

The Assistant Commissioner stood on the platform and stared in. He gripped his stick and listened for Crosse's

81

coming. He did not believe that the man would shoot, but he was a little disturbed by the flow of sweet words. The man stood before a mirror buttoning a jacket with a high collar across a great naked chest, tufted between the breasts with red hair. The Assistant Commissioner was puzzled for a moment at the blue braided uniform, but then he noticed on a chair a cap with a red band. 'I've been as big a sinner as any of you. But I've come to Jesus and I've been forgiven.' The Assistant Commissioner swung his stick, listening for the feet upon the stairs, and the man moved and pursed his lips and turned his head to see that he was clean behind the ears. When he spoke he circled his lips as if to whistle, and the words popped out one by one like little sticky sweets.

'Oh, if you only knew, friends, the sweetness of forgiveness, the balm, the peace.' It was impossible to doubt his sincerity. He was as sincere as the actor-manager aware for an act, for a scene, for a soliloquy's length, of the slings and arrows of outrageous fortune, before the packed stalls and the respectful 'gods'.

'When you feel the flames of Hell, friends, tearing at your heart, don't say, "It's too late". Then's the moment to come to Jesus, and oh, the balm of it and the peace.'

The Assistant Commissioner wondered: Has he locked the door? He'll break for the window. Where's he put his revolver?

'I've felt the flames, but I've been forgiven, I've felt the flames, but I feel the peace.' He held back his lips and examined his teeth and gums, while his voice absent-mindedly hummed: 'Peace and balm, peace and balm.' He drew a loose match from his pocket and picked his teeth, then rubbed them up and down with his handkerchief. 'Peace and balm, peace and balm,' he said, buttoning up his pockets, laying large plump hands across his scalp, smoothing the brossed reddish hair with a bishop's benedictory and confirming touch.

Somebody outside pulled at the door.

The man turned; peace and balm withered on his lips. 'Who's that?' Nobody troubled to answer, but the lock shook and shivered. The Salvationist turned to the window and saw in the splash of light on the steel platform the Assistant Commissioner swinging his stick in his right hand, his legs a little apart expecting a charge. Before the lock broke he was at his bed, fumbling under the pillow; while the door poised ajar before the crash, he was back at the window with the revolver pointed. 'Get off that escape.'

The Assistant Commissioner watched him, swung his stick, saw for a moment not the brossed hair and the fat desperate face, but an old woman, who had been too close with her money, raising her hands and screaming, while the steam from Paddington Station rose across the window and a goods train plodding down to Westbourne Grove hooted on a higher note than she could reach, so that no one heard her; any more than later the couple who lived below had heard the dreadful little sounds of sawing.

'Get off that – ' but the door was open and he swung to meet it, unable to make up his mind at whom to shoot, still dithering and undecided when the handcuffs were on his wrists. The Assistant Commissioner climbed in through the open window, Jenks examined the gun with curiosity, weighing it in his hand, opening the magazine, Crosse put the key of the cuffs in his pocket and said: 'You're under arrest on a charge of murdering Mrs Janet Crowle at Paddington on the 4th. Anything you say – '

Jenks said: 'It's a 1916 type. They're slow on the trigger.'

'Come on,' Crosse said, 'put on his cap.' The room was full of men picking things up. Somebody put the cap on the man's head. 'Collins, you stay and clear up with Jenks,' Crosse said. He pushed the man between the shoulders so that he stumbled. 'Get on, can't you. You'll be keeping us up late enough as it is.' The man lowered himself painfully down the stairs as if he had been beaten. 'You ought to be ashamed,' he said, 'hitting me.' He began to speak again in an undertone of Jesus and how he had been forgiven. 'Holy martyrs,' he said, and on the bottom step, 'company of the blessed.' He was impregnably entrenched against shame or retribution; he was touched only by a little momentary fear.

'Are you coming back to the Yard, sir?' Crosse asked.

'No,' the Assistant Commissioner said. 'No. I'll see your report in the morning. I want to look, to look through the Streatham papers tonight.' He drew his coat carefully past the splintered woodwork and remembered what the secretary had said, sipping sherry in the Berkeley, 'It's a battlefield.' But he had been referring to something else, the Assistant Commissioner could not remember what. I suppose, he thought, this is a victory, but there's no such thing as a decisive victory. He looked at his watch and calculated that he might perhaps allow himself twenty minutes for a little food before he sat down to the Streatham papers; the time would not be quite wasted, over his food he could consider Drover.

3

MR SURROGATE rose later than usual. At 8.30 Davis came
in and drew the blinds, and a flow of pale autumnal sun
filled the wash-basin and spread across the bed. Mr Surrogate grunted and turned on his side. He did not wake
again until eleven.

The machines in the match factory stopped working for
five minutes while everyone drank a glass of milk and pretended to eat a dry water biscuit. Some slipped it into their
pockets to throw away in the lavatory at lunch time, others
dropped it on the floor among the litter of discarded
boxes.

Conder sucked a sweet and stared into the melancholy
future. 'Take this to the subs,' he said, and watched his exclusive story disappear in the hands of a messenger down the
stairs; soon it would be leaden type and soon a column of
print, and twenty-four hours later it would be pulp. It did not
seem fair to Conder that the products of his brain should be
condemned to the same cycle as his body. Something should
be left. His body must decay, but some permanent echo
should remain of the defective bathroom, the child with
whooping cough. He began to write, again without thinking:
'Reds clash behind locked Doors'. No story left his hands
with the truth unheightened. Condemned to the recording of
trivialities, he saw the only hope of a posthumous immor-
tality in a picturesque lie which might catch a historian's
notice as it lay buried in an old file.

Mr Surrogate rolled on to his back, opened his eyes and

met his wife's wide innocent gaze. The picture did her more than justice, for she had not been beautiful and she had not been innocent. Mr Surrogate could not have endured a realistic portrait on the wall, but he was sometimes able to persuade himself that this was the essential woman, that now she was not malicious and adroit and knowledgeable, that now she understood him as he wanted to be understood. While he dressed he told the portrait that it was not every widower who would refrain from bedding with an attractive and willing girl out of respect for a dead woman. He used the term 'bedding' for its Anglo-Saxon flavour, he had no use for Gallic flippancy; 'she would certainly have bedded with me', he told himself and had a momentary vision of flaxen-haired warriors tumbling earnestly upon rushes before departing to their curved boats. He remembered that he had made an appointment with her for the afternoon and decided that he would notice the effect upon her intelligent but uncultivated brain of the new abstract film at the Academy. 'She is worth studying,' he informed his wife, who dangled with propriety on the wall.

If she could only stay there, and in the small engraved casket at Golders Green ('with love for the wife and homage to the artist'), but she leapt at him from every wall of Caroline Bury's drawing-room. He was alone for three minutes with her; nowhere to turn, nowhere to look; this she had painted in Greenwich Park, this at Antibes; he could remember the very occasion in Cornwall when this picture had composed itself in her mind, and she had left him immediately to make a note of it; he had complained afterwards in a letter to Mrs Bury that she did not respect his manhood. Now in the rather dim and shrouded room he turned with real agony to meet the only person left alive who knew him thoroughly, to whom in past years he had confessed all his hesitations and indeterminacies, his meannesses and studied generosities, his intellectual chaos. 'How are you, Caroline?

How long it is,' but he winced and withdrew from the recognition of time passing, time greying the hair, making the body less agile and the brain more hopeless.

Caroline Bury advanced into the room with an air of vagueness and distinction. She gave an impression of not knowing whom she might find in her own house, what curious personality would speak from between the bric-à-brac with which the rooms were a little overcrowded. Her haggard sunken face would have had its beauty recognized at once on an ancient fresco or an Eastern tomb, but in a theatre or a bookshop or a modern street it was likely to arouse only curiosity; Mr Surrogate had never seen her outside her home.

She peered at him shortsightedly and grated a greeting in a voice full of discords, but again the hearer had to recognize that in another age and in another continent this sound like the scraping of metal discs, might have been thought beautiful. 'I want to talk to you before the others come.' In her brain Mr Surrogate knew were stored all his wife's letters, but though he was embarrassed and embittered by the knowledge, he could not resist the compliment of her interest. After all, in this room Henry James had constructed his sentences like Chinese boxes which held at the centre a tiny colloquialism; Wilde had unloosed a torrent of epigrams; Hardy had wondered what it was all about.

'Tell me about Drover.'

Mr Surrogate had spoken of enlisting her interest; he had known, at the time, that was unnecessary. Listening to the writers round her table, Caroline Bury appeared to have a passion for literature, listening to the politicians she seemed the last of the political hostesses; those who knew her well were aware that literature and politics were only the territories in which she had chosen to exercise her passion for charity, a charity that was satirical, practical to the point of cynicism, the kind of charity which no man was too proud or vain to refuse.

He told her all he knew, humbly, a little grudgingly, watching the wheels of a fine intellect beginning to turn. He was jealous. Beneath Drover's story, buried only just beneath the succeeding words, 'policeman – wife – Hyde Park – appeal', buried so shallowly that between the phrases scraps of the old bones showed plain ('It reminds me . . . by the way . . . you remember'), lay his own tale, the first example he knew of Caroline Bury's passion to help.

'Of course I remember. But go on. I want to hear about Drover.'

The grey sea lapped the shingle and the rain drummed on the asphalt promenade. Mr Surrogate, a much thinner and much younger Mr Surrogate, walked up and down in the rain talking to himself, a telegram crumpled in his hand. He had been married six months and he had no money and his wife was ill in London and the doctor said that she must go south. He returned wet to the skin to Justin Bury's house, where he was spending the week-end, and at lunch he had broken down, shivering and sneezing and weeping. It was his first complete humiliation, and when in later years he had humiliated himself again and again, Mr Surrogate himself could not have said how far he was influenced by the knowledge of how well it had paid the first time. Caroline Bury had sent them both to Hyères. Soon after that Justin died, of a cold, during the hot summer of 1921, in Spain.

'Do you remember your house by the sea?'

'Of course I do. But go on. How old is his wife?' When he had finished, Caroline Bury said with a high bird-like screech of amazement and disbelief: 'But it's absurd. They can't hang him. A fit of temper.'

'On Thursday,' Mr Surrogate said.

'Too absurd. We must do something. I'll ask the C.I.D.

man – what's he called? – the Assistant Commissioner to lunch.'

'Do you know everyone, Caroline?'

'I haven't seen him since he came back from the East. But we were very dear friends once. Of course he's incredibly pompous.'

'He won't be able to do anything.'

'My dear Philip, don't be so defeatist. The whole thing is absurd and therefore something can be done.' Mr Surrogate opened his lips to protest against this assumption that life of its nature was not absurd, but cleared his throat instead. What was the good? Caroline Bury had Faith. He was not quite certain in what she had faith, whether in the God of the Jews, of Rome, of Canterbury, of Mrs Eddy or of Mrs Besant, but however vague her faith, it was unshakable; perhaps it was unshakable because of its vagueness. It was useless to disprove the divinity of Christ, for then it would be found that this was not one of the articles of her belief. She could waive the divinity of Christ, she could waive the Old Testament and the Gospels and the Acts. She could waive the Koran, she could even waive the sacred books of India; these were minor points. She had Faith.

'The Assistant Commissioner's got nothing to do with – '

'He'll know the right people to talk to. If only the Labour Government was still in, I'd have had the Home Secretary to lunch. But Beale. I don't know anything about Beale.'

'He's a temperance maniac.'

'He's a nonentity. I'm not interested in nonentities.'

A faint smile wavered across Mr Surrogate's face and he smoothed his hair. Shoes creaked on the parquet outside. Caroline Bury said: 'I expect this is Crabbe. Do you know Crabbe?'

'No,' Mr Surrogate said, 'no. His works of course.'

'He's been very tiresome since they gave him the O.M.'

Almost immediately the room was full of people.

At lunch Crabbe sat opposite him, an old man with a white moustache and red aggrieved eyes. He had not written a book for ten years and he was universally admired. But he was firmly convinced that people were 'getting at' him. Although he was known to be difficult, he was still invited everywhere, partly because of his reputation and the Order of Merit, partly because once, five years ago, he had talked brilliantly and maliciously all through lunch. Hostesses always believed that it might happen again at any moment.

Crabbe was silent, but Sean Cassidy, the poet, was not. He talked continuously at one end of the table about astrology. The preliminary difficulty of understanding the ideas of Zoroaster was not made easier by Cassidy's brogue. But he had his uses. He prevented the general conversation being killed by the loud, clear, faintly American accents of two critics who were discussing the ideas of a Swedish theologian.

Mr Surrogate, aware that Crabbe was watching him with an inflamed eye, began to talk about the League of Nations with the quiet young woman beside him. 'I believed in it once,' he said and admitted a moment later, 'it is perhaps a useful start towards the World State.'

'Under the Hammer and Sickle?' the young woman asked. Mr Surrogate smiled approvingly and sipped his Hock. He tried to see through Crabbe to the clock behind him. In half an hour Kay would be waiting for him. The wine made him feel young and vigorous. Thank God, he thought, I am not old like Crabbe and past my time; young women still hang on my words. 'Yes, the Hammer and Sickle,' but catching the next moment Caroline Bury's eye, he plunged into humility. I am lecherous, conceited, mean, cowardly; he would have liked to confess to his neighbour all the shabby history of his marriage, to expose himself bare of intellectual and moral pretences, and what would be left? A man, Mr Surrogate thought, revolving his wine glass, no better than a criminal waiting execution, but none the less, he thought, his spirit soaring again on its perpetual seesaw, so that his fellow-guests sank swiftly below him and were flattened out among the plates, a man, the essential I.

Crabbe cleared his throat and everybody, except Cassidy, fell abruptly silent, listening. He cleared his throat again and began to choke. 'Gristle,' somebody said, and his neighbour patted his back. 'Porphyry,' Cassidy said, 'writing of the Sign of Cancer. . . .' Crabbe gulped and was suddenly better, but his neighbour continued absent-mindedly to pat him on the back. Crabbe glared malignantly; it was quite obvious that he thought he was being 'got at'. Everybody began talking again. Mr Surrogate said: 'Under certain circumstances, I should be ready to put up with Geneva as a stop-gap.'

'The moon in Virgo rules the bowels and belly.'

'His treatment of the Unitarians.'

'If Geneva,' Mr Surrogate said, 'broadcast brotherhood as often as it broadcasts hate – '

Crabbe leant forward across the table and cleared his throat. Everyone fell silent, listening. Crabbe regarded Mr Surrogate with venom. His old eyes swelled and contracted. 'Geneva,' he said, 'I've never heard Geneva – ' He seemed at a loss for words, a little bewildered by this sudden incursion into contemporary life from his background of long Norfolk fields, low sea and tall empty churches. But everyone listened intently and humbly to hear what the creator of Dinah Cullen and Joseph Sentry and the mad Corbett had to say about Geneva. 'I've heard Moscow,' Crabbe said, 'I've heard Rome, I've heard New York, but I can't get Geneva. What's your set?' he spat out furiously at Mr Surrogate.

'Really,' Mr Surrogate said, 'I'm sorry. You mis-understood. I wasn't referring – '

'Don't tell me tales about a Crystal,' Crabbe said. 'I may be old, but I'm not daft yet. The tales people tell me about what they get with a Crystal.'

Mr Surrogate sighed with relief, going down the steps, hearing the eighteenth-century door close behind him. That was over. He had done his best. Now he could leave everything to Caroline Bury. After business pleasure, but he was a little put out to find that Kay was not waiting for him at Oxford Circus. He bought an evening paper, but there was little in it but lists of starters and in the stop-press the results of the 2.30. All down Oxford Street the shops were closed and the street was almost empty. Little groups of people up from the country passed back and forth along the north side staring into the windows at models with black cloth faces. Mr Surrogate looked at his watch and bought another paper. 'The Paddington Murder. Flying Squad Raid near Euston. Man Detained.' Curious the interest in crime, Mr Surrogate thought, and turned to another column. 'Drama at Red Meeting. Clash behind Locked Doors.' He read the account to the end. How these pressmen exaggerated; a little fracas, worn nerves, bad temper. He turned the page: 'Mr MacDonald Presents Golf Trophy. The Royal and Ancient Game. A Lossiemouth Welcome.'

*

Milly laid the newspaper open on her dressing-table while she put on her hat. Mrs Coney watched her from between the hairbrushes with frigid disapproval. Had the photograph been taken after her husband's death? If so there was no hint of grief. Perhaps it was an old photograph, and Milly tried to imagine what kind of a wife she had been, but the cameo brooch daunted her. It was like a medal granted for some piece of inhuman rectitude. Her hair pulled back into a knot above a waste of brow, she was of the same stuff as the women who gladly 'gave' their sons to war and fought in parish councils for marble memorials. The face filled Milly with despair.

Her voice was hollow with it down the telephone wire.

Conrad Drover did not recognize her, laying down his pen, his eyes still following a column of figures along the sheet. 'Who's that? Speak up, please, I can't hear you.' It was his chief clerk's voice. It had no relation to his character, it was formed defensively to rebuke office boys who stole his india-rubber, to answer the questions of the Board.

'I only wanted to speak to Mr Drover.'

'Speaking.'

'Oh, Conrad, is it you?' He recognized the voice then, glanced quickly through the glass door at the bent backs of the clerks, behind him at the door of the manager's room; he was alone between the glass walls, isolated between his superiors and his subordinates. 'Yes, Milly, what is it?' It was hard to shed his clerk's voice quickly, his tongue still tingled with figures, he knew that he sounded impatient.

'I only wanted to tell you. When Kay came home. She said . . .'

'Is the party doing anything?'

'They are all signing the petition. But, Conrad, listen. Something else. Mr Surrogate's helping. He's speaking to a lady who has influence.'

'Listen, Milly.' He bent close over the telephone and confided to it his deep mistrust. 'Don't believe too much in what they'll do. Strangers. They are interested for a time, but if things don't go right, they lose interest. It doesn't mean anything to them. We've got to do it all ourselves.' Through the door in front of him he could hear very faintly the scratching of the clerks' pens; somebody was reading out a row of figures; when he looked round, the shadow of the manager darkened the door behind, moving up and down, droning to a dictaphone. 'We're alone.'

'I'm on the way to that woman now.'

'I'll see you tonight, Milly.'

'I was wondering – I suppose it's impossible – you couldn't come with me?'

'If you could wait till lunch time.'

'I daren't wait. Can't you get away an hour earlier?'

'I wish I could.' He put his head on his hands and stared at the sheets of paper on his desk; the little black figures rose at him like swarming flies. 'It's impossible.' He heard the sound of the receiver replaced and silence sweeping up the wire. He was alone again with men whom he disliked and mistrusted, above all mistrusted. Even the most inefficient clerk, he felt certain, was scheming for his place; his glass room was a tiny raft of security round which they all swam hoping to dislodge him, hoping to catch him asleep; his position was easier, but he had not their quality of eternal vigilance and concentrated cunning; other things clamoured for his attention, his brother in prison, Milly going up the suburban street in fear and despair. But he did not even trust Milly; she loved his brother, he supposed, as much as he did himself; any word of encouragement or affection she gave him was for his brother's sake.

But as she walked up the long suburban hill lined with little half-timbered houses with chocolate-coloured cornices: 'Desirable Residence. Only £50 down', she was not afraid. She was brave because suddenly she was angry. It wasn't right how things were, that Conrad shouldn't be allowed an hour or two to help his brother. She tugged hard at a bell and to the small grey woman who answered the door she said furiously: 'I want Mrs Coney.'

'I'm Mrs Coney.'

Milly looked at her with astonishment and saw now the cameo brooch, the grey hair pulled back from the forehead, the black high-necked dress, but what the newspaper had failed to indicate was the smallness of the scale; she was no more than an imitation in miniature of the harsh and unbearable woman.

'I'm sorry. Could I speak to you?'

'I don't know, I'm sure, whether I've the time. Are you

the Press?' The eyes, bewildered and hunted, peered over Milly's shoulder, flinched in dread of a battery of cameras, of tripods, of microphones. Milly thought: She's as weak as water. She doesn't know where to turn. She's afraid of me. I can do what I like with her. She said gently, as if it were her part to encourage and to soothe: 'I'm Mrs Drover.'

'Yes? Yes?' The name had conveyed absolutely nothing.

'My husband's in prison.'

Milly could see Mrs Coney drawing up a little courage like a bucket from a deep and drying well. She began to close the door. 'I'm sorry,' she said. 'I've no washing – or mending. I do it all myself.'

Milly put her foot in the door. 'You don't understand. It was my husband who killed –'

Mrs Coney backed against a carved wooden bear which held two umbrellas in its outstretched arms. 'Oh.'

'I wanted to talk to you,' Milly said. She followed her into the narrow hall and closed the door behind her. Mrs Coney looked up at her with sudden bright relief and said: 'I thought it was the Press again. I couldn't stand – have they been at you, too?'

'No. My man's still alive, you see.' Milly, five feet four inches high, towered over the woman.

Mrs Coney said nervously: 'You'll have a cup of tea. Excuse the untidiness. I've been cleaning up.'

One side of the passage was packed with occasional tables. Two or three ferns stood on the floor and the carpet had been taken up. The air was full of floating dust. 'Would you mind the kitchen?' Milly noticed everywhere the signs of a fussing and incompetent woman, a woman who drives the dust from one room to settle in another, who buys Danish eggs for economy and leaves the gas burning.

Milly said with sudden anger: 'I haven't come here to say I'm sorry.'

95

Mrs Coney whipped round from the gas stove, kettle in hand, scattering drops over the linoleum. She said in a frightened voice: 'It must have been all a mistake. I'm not blaming you.' She put the spluttering kettle back on the stove and began to drop tea into the pot.

'He was only defending me.'

'I'm sure he was.'

'You've put in six spoonfuls.'

'Oh, dear, it will be strong. Do you mind it strong?' She sat on the other side of the kitchen table staring at Milly with her little finger crooked away from the teacup. 'You're older than your husband?' Milly asked.

'Ten years,' Mrs Coney said. She said weakly: 'I always thought he'd catch me up, that I'd be gone first. I didn't think I'd ever be left alone.'

'It feels odd, doesn't it?' Milly said.

'Odd? I keep on going into rooms and coming out again. I can't settle. Would you like a piece of cake, dear?'

'It's good of you,' Milly said, 'treating me like this,' but she knew that Mrs Coney's goodness, her white brow and cameo brooch and air of frightened rectitude, meant nothing at all. It was only her surroundings which lent her an air of positive virtue. Mrs Coney was encircled by death and crime and implacable justice; even pallor and hesitation and a commonplace kindliness gained dignity from those surroundings.

'I was so afraid it was the Press, dear. They brought great noisy cameras and told me to speak to them. They said they were going to put me on the films,' Mrs Coney said with pale astonishment, thinking of campuses and cocktail parties and orgies in Imperial Rome.

'What did you say?'

'I didn't know what to say. So they told me to say something about demanding justice,' Mrs Coney added with an air of shame and fear, peering at Milly over the brim of her cup and blowing on the tea to cool it. It occurred to Milly how easily the whole affair could have been settled between them. Mrs Coney did not want vengeance, she did not want another woman's husband slaughtered because she had lost her own; they were two women of the same class who could talk things over and come to an understanding. It was gentlefolk who had broken in with the laws they had made themselves, earning the fees they had fixed themselves, hundreds of pounds going into their pockets while the trial went on. A death for a death – the law demanded this, but the law had not been made by Jim or Mrs Coney or herself, it had been made by kings and priests and lawyers and rich men. Sometimes they let you off, but the decision would not be made by Mrs Coney; again, it would be the politicians and the lawyers who knew nothing about the man they saved and cared less. Somewhere, at some time, in a newspaper or a book, Milly had read the words, 'Judgement by your peers'. She had thought it meant judgement by your lords and had been laughed at for thinking so, 'It means judgement by your equals', but where, she asked now of Mrs Coney, was a judge who was their equal, a man with three pounds a week, who lived as they lived? And the jury? Tradesmen and gentlemen. It wasn't fair, Milly said, with her tea and Mrs Coney and the long walk home forgotten in a sense of stifled injustice.

'It's the law,' Mrs Coney said, blowing into her tea with her little finger crooked.

'They're hanging him on Thursday.'

'I'm so sorry, dear,' said Mrs Coney. She was inadequate to anything but submission. 'Arthur was always hot-tempered. He hit me sometimes.' Her small jet eyes closed for a moment and she gripped the edge of the table as though with an intolerable longing for a blow.

'I've brought a petition paper,' Milly said. 'Will you sign it?'

Mrs Coney's eyes flashed open. She was suspicious and defensive. 'I don't like signing things. What does it say?'

'You don't want me to read all the rigmarole,' Milly said. 'It's asking the King not to have Jim hanged.'

Mrs Coney's shoulders twitched, her chin went back, and she raised the teapot. 'I don't like to trouble His Majesty,' she said. 'He's got enough to think of. Some more tea, dear?'

'He won't see it,' Milly patiently explained. 'It goes to one of those people in Parliament.'

'I don't like signing things,' Mrs Coney repeated. 'Arthur never liked me signing things. If you sign things when people come to the door (I don't mean you, dear), you don't know what you let yourself in for – vacuum cleaners, wireless, bedroom suites. Arthur always said, never put your name to a printed form.'

'I'm not selling anything,' Milly said. 'You can read it all if you like.'

'Oh, I'm not accusing you, dear, but it just makes one careful. I can't read it without my glasses.'

'Let me read it to you then.'

'Couldn't you leave it behind and I'd ask Arthur's brother, and then I'd post it to you?'

'No,' Milly said, 'there isn't time. Listen. You don't want Jim to be hanged?'

'He ought to be punished,' Mrs Coney said.

'Oh, he'll be punished all right. Eighteen years in prison. Don't you call that punishment?'

'I don't like to *sign* anything without asking Arthur's brother. But you can tell them that I don't want him hung.'

'That's not enough. Please, Mrs Coney,' but she realized too late that begging would get nothing from the meek suspicious woman. Mrs Coney for the first time in her life was tasting power. Though submission had always satisfied her, there was something in the novel taste which thinned her lips. But she could not fight straightforwardly. Her spirit, like a mole, burrowed circuitously in darkness, emerging at unsuspected places. 'I don't believe in interfering with the law.'

'This isn't interfering with the law. It's got nothing to do with his politics. Don't think I'm a Red. If he hadn't been one, he wouldn't be in trouble now.'

'What? Is he a Red? I wouldn't raise a finger to save a Red.' It was odd to hear somebody you knew as well as your own body labelled with the same badge as a lot of other men. Milly protested: 'He's never done anybody any harm.'

'Oh, but if he's a Red. They want to take everything away from us. You oughtn't to have asked me. You ought to have known better. Thieves.' Mrs Coney glared round the kitchen, noting everything which she feared to lose – the silver-plated napkin-rings, the christening-mug on a shelf, the carved Swiss bread-board, and through the door, in the passage, the ferns and the wooden bear and the two umbrellas, but yet beneath the fear and the hate, the same inner submissiveness, so that anyone watching her might know that they could steal with impunity. She would hate them, their hands on the rings; she would talk at them, the Swiss bread-board in their sack; but she would never fight for her possessions.

Milly said: 'You've got to sign.'

Mrs Coney replied stubbornly with one hand spread over the top of the teapot: 'I'd do nothing for a Red.' She was as unconcerned by argument as a dead woman, a woman happy dead, who feared the removal of the nails which pinned down her coffin-lid. 'They want to take everything. One's not safe.'

'He's your own class,' Milly said.

'He's not my class. My Arthur would have been an inspector one day.' Her dead Arthur climbed and climbed through the otherwise empty space of her mind, his uniform changing as he climbed, first stripes appearing, then braid. Presently his helmet vanished and a cap appeared – the making of a man.

'Then you won't sign?'

'No. At least – not until I've spoken to Arthur's brother.' She jumped as a small bell ping-pinged above her head. She had never got accustomed to the suddenness of an electric bell; in the old days the quiver of the wire all down a passage gave warning. 'Oh,' she said, 'dear, won't you answer it?'

'Who is it?'

'I can't bear their cameras,' Mrs Coney said. 'Send them away. I've got nothing to tell them.' She remembered, pleading with Milly through her small eyes, which had no more expression than a pair of jet bugles, the day of her husband's death and how the news had been told her at the door in a polite, kind, patronizing voice, while before she could recover and recognize the tripods on the pavement her bewilderment and horror had been caught by their lenses and reproduced as staring stupidity. 'Tell them I'm not in.'

Milly got up. All down the passage she thought hard; she waited for a moment beside the wooden bear and then opened the door. A man with a bald head took off his hat and said: 'Mrs Coney?'

'Wait there,' Milly said and turned down the passage. He followed her quickly, walking on the tips of patent shoes. She rounded on him and he watched her, hat in hand, with an expression of persistent humility. 'I said wait there.' Milly knew that her voice had nearly broken. If she could not win her battle soon, she would give in; she was not used to fighting, she had always relied on Jim to do the fighting, putting out drunken neighbours, pushing a path for both of them through the crowd at fun fairs.

'Excuse me,' the man said softly, turning on his heel. 'I

misunderstood' – walking back to the door; but Milly was aware, when he stopped for a moment by the bear and tapped it on the skull with his knuckles, of his interior hardness; this was what one laid oneself open to when one became news, soft-spoken strangers in the house who touched and felt and criticized and never said a word of what they thought.

She closed the kitchen door behind her and said: 'It's a newspaper man.'

'Did you tell him I was out? Has he gone?'

'I told him to wait.'

'Why do you hate me?' Mrs Coney said and began to cry. She sat bolt upright in her chair, her eyes as expressionless as ever; like the plaster cast of a statue to rectitude with water dripping down the face. She took out a gay lace handkerchief and dabbed at her cheeks.

'When you've signed this. I'll send him away.'

'He won't go.'

'I'll make him,' Milly said.

'You're a wicked woman. I haven't a pen.'

'Here's a pencil.'

'I believe you planned it all.'

'Oh no,' Milly said. 'I'm not that clever. It's luck. It's the first luck I've had since your man tried to hit me.' She began to cry herself with bitter joy, seeing the scrawl across the printed form, 'Rose Coney', thinking I've done something for him, I've fought for him, I've been of use to him, full of gratitude suddenly to Conrad, who had helped her to this relief, grateful to all the world except Jim's enemies. 'I'd do as much for you,' she said, 'if I could. But your man's dead. He can't be helped. Mine can. There's nothing I wouldn't do.'

The man was back in the passage. He had picked up a vase and was looking at its underside. 'Mrs Coney?' he asked again.

'No. She won't see you.'

'I don't mind waiting.'

'I shouldn't wait if I were you. You may miss a story if you wait.'

'Oh, I'm used to waiting,' he said. He became confidential, while he moved up and down in the hall, lifted a pot of ferns, tapped a vase, put his finger in the bear's mouth. 'I've never got anything in any other way.' He raised a face like a square façade with all the windows shuttered, life hidden from the street, going on in twilight in the quiet rooms. 'Would she mind if I smoked?' He lit a cigarette and stroked a green leaf. 'She ought to give them tea. This bear came from Switzerland. Cunning little teeth it's got.' He spoke in a sad quiet way. 'I've seen a room of these things. Everything's carved wood. At the Schaffhausen falls. They all played a tune too. Wastepaper bins, cigarette boxes, chairs, fruit dishes. And the cuckoo clocks cuckooing all the time.'

'Aren't you going?'

'I'm used to waiting. I shouldn't be surprised if this bear played a tune if one knew how.' He rapped it again on the skull.

'I've got to go,' Milly said, but the man fascinated her. He had told the truth when he said that he was used to waiting. He was so practised in waiting that he seemed to want nothing else but to stand there feeling things and talking to anyone who would listen. But he was not sociable. It was only one way of passing the time. He was not thinking about her, but of something quite different. If I were not here, she thought, he would sit down and go to sleep.

'Ah,' the man said, 'I've got it.' He picked one of the umbrellas from the bear's embrace and a musical box in the bear's belly began to play a very simple jingly tune. 'It brings it all back,' the man said, not troubling to raise his voice; she could only hear what he said when the tune sank a little.

102

'Disappointed – long drive – wet – without a handkerchief – three shillings for tea – no lavatory.'

Milly said: 'But you must go. I promised that you'd go.' The tune came to an end, the cylinder of the musical box whining and grinding in the wooden stomach. 'Nobody can steal your umbrella anyway,' the man said, beginning to prowl again. 'Now is this the late Mr Coney?'

Milly said: 'I'm Mrs Drover.'

He showed no surprise. 'You know Mrs Coney?'

'No, but I came here to ask her to sign the petition.'

He watched her, his eyes round and melancholy and uninterested. He gave the impression that all human stories were often repeated and that it was his unfortunate fate to listen to every repetition. 'Ah, you've got nerve, and did she?'

'I'll tell you that if you'll come away with me.'

He put on his hat, gave the bear a final rap and opened the door. 'She ought to give those ferns tea.' Without turning to see whether Milly was following him, he began to walk down the hill between the chocolate-coloured residences. 'Perhaps I'll call back and tell her so, and perhaps I won't. Her story's dead. No more interest. Don't think I can offer you any money for an interview. I can't. The manager would have a fit. That's a nice house there.'

Milly followed a little behind him. Her achievement shrank with every pace he took. 'I don't know what paper you are,' she said. 'But I can try another one. I don't want money anyway.'

He became brusque. 'Ah, you're another one of them. "All I want is justice." *All*, think of that. As if justice were a pound of tea, as if it existed anywhere, as if – '

'I don't want justice,' Milly said. 'I've seen enough of it. I was in Court every day.'

He stopped and leant against an estate agent's board and watched her with a thin flicker of interest. 'And did she sign the petition?'

'I'm not going to tell you unless you're interested,' Milly said. 'I want publicity.'

'Is that all?' he asked sarcastically, but she did not recognize his sarcasm. The world to her still seemed a simple place; one wanted things and they were given or denied, one was happy or unhappy, loved or hated. She had lived at one remove; she had never been close enough to life to see the confusing details, to learn that one was miserably happy, that a giving was sometimes a denial, that one loved and hated for the same reasons. 'Yes, that's all,' she said. Publicity for the moment was all she wanted; she would have surrendered money if she had had it, health if it had been required of her, friends if she had had them. 'I'll go to another paper,' she said.

'You're too innocent to be about alone,' he said. 'They won't be any more interested than I am. You may as well tell me. It'll be worth a paragraph, I daresay. Perhaps two. I'll squeeze it in somewhere, I promise you.'

'Will you write it out, the promise?' He laughed at her as he leant back against the notice board, blocking out some of the large white capitals 'To Let' with his hat, and again she was troubled by a sense of complexity because he did not seem to be laughing at her but at himself. She wished that she had Kay with her to deal with him. As the thought crossed her mind, he surprised her by saying, 'I'd never have recognized you. You aren't a bit like your sister.'

'Do you know Kay?' She added quickly, 'It's not that I wouldn't trust you, but I daren't take a chance. You see, it's for my husband.'

'Oh,' he said, 'I'm not offended. But your sister would know that writing a thing doesn't make it any more true. You're talking to a man who knows.'

He watched her. She was puzzled and disheartened. She didn't know what he was talking about.

'What a fool,' he said, 'to go and get into trouble and lose a nice girl like you.'

'It wasn't his fault. We were happy. It doesn't pay to be happy. I always told him it couldn't go on, but somehow we couldn't help it.'

'My name's Conder.'

'Mine's Milly.'

Conder said: 'Come and have some coffee with me in town. Then you can tell me about Mrs Coney. I'll do my best for you. I really will. I'm a married man myself. I'd like to talk to you about my kids. One's got whooping cough. Inconvenient because we've just moved into a new house.' He began to walk rapidly down the hill towards the bus stop, talking and talking, of the wife, of the children; he escaped in a torrent of words from a Swiss umbrella-stand, and from the girl who laughed at him ten years ago by the Schaffhausen falls – 'You funny little man,' as he grabbed at her dress in the summer-house (one franc to see the falls through green and pink and mauve glass) while the multi-coloured water foamed and rocked outside and the cuckoo clocks sounded from the chalet and all the fruit dishes played tunes. He complained of his fictitious comfort, spoke bitterly of his fabulous happiness, and by the time the pirate bus had swerved to the kerb and away again with its contraband cargo, his discontent was as unreal as his world.

In Regent Street there was a traffic block for half a mile. Looking back they could see the line of buses stretching to Oxford Circus. There was a crowd on the pavement, and a scarlet cloth was being laid down outside a cinema. Stalwart women guarded it on either side with their hats a little awry and their hands hugging black bags from which they had eaten their lunch. They were flushed and cross and excited and suspicious that someone might push in from behind.

'Business at a standstill,' said Conder. Mounted police backed their horses at the edge of the pavement, keeping the road clear. 'If you wanted to buy something, you couldn't. If you wanted to meet a man on business, you couldn't. We'll be sitting here now for a quarter of an hour. Patience,' Conder said, 'you've got to be patient. This is a State occasion. The Queen's going to a talkie.' The street shone in the sun, empty all the way to Piccadilly Circus; after a shower of rain the pavements steamed. An old-fashioned Daimler hummed gently round the curve of the Quadrant, and men in morning coats bowed from the hips. Then a high head of hair in a grey toque passed into the cinema. Somebody dropped a paper bag on the carpet and there was a thin sound of cheering. All the engines of all the buses started simultaneously, the mounted policemen cantered away along the empty street, and everybody began to talk. It was like the end of the two minutes' silence on Armistice Day.

*

Conrad Drover's voice was high with indignation. He told the clerks one by one what he thought of them, not forgetting the young man, a nephew of the managing director, who was learning the business from the bottom. He wore a light suit and a public-school tie. 'If I'm not here to keep an eye on every one of you.' The young man stared back insolently. He smelt of money. A motoring paper was open on his desk; often through his glass door Conrad had heard his low penetrating voice telling the other clerks of his week-end at Brighton. 'You aren't worth your pay. Don't get the idea you're indispensable – ' They stared back at him, and he became suddenly afraid of the phalanx of hostile eyes and dived back into his room.

It was one o'clock, but he went on tidying his papers until the clerks' room was empty. His fingers were trembling and he felt a little weak at the knees. He knew that he was hated and he hated them all in return as schemers. If they could see a way, they would make capital even out of his brother's condemnation. He wondered sometimes whether this would go on all through his life, fresh relays of clerks, fresh relays of intriguers for his place. It was always the same, he told himself, a chief clerk was never popular, but other men perhaps were strong enough to stay the course. They had some source of fresh strength. 'I'm tired out,' he said aloud, and his knuckles drummed on his desk. The sound woke him from introspection, the clerks' room was empty now, but the shadow of the manager still passed to and fro behind his glass door; it wasn't safe giving way even for a moment. If the manager heard him talking aloud with no one in the room, he might begin to mistrust him, his figures and his discipline; he might decide that it was time to try the director's nephew. Conrad was quite certain that one day that would happen. Meanwhile one must be calm, develop habits, think of other things, not take the office always home with one, balance-sheets and incompetent clerks and the director's nephew locked in the skull as securely as papers in a safe of which the combination has been lost.

He picked his hat from a peg, his umbrella from a stand, his attaché case from the desk. It was five minutes later than his usual hour for leaving the office, and it was possible that his table at the restaurant would have been taken by a stranger.

As he passed through the clerks' room he saw an evening paper spread out conspicuously on the desk of the director's nephew. It was a day old and open at the account of his brother's appeal. There was a smudgy photograph of his brother taken on the day of his wedding. He wore a stiff collar and a dark tie, and the unaccustomed clothes brought out a likeness to Conrad. Conrad's heart jolted. He was afraid that the manager would see it. He crumpled it into a ball and threw it into the wastepaper basket. But the manager might want something to read at lunch and pick it out again. If I could burn it, he thought, and felt his pocket for matches. But there was no fireplace. When he heard the manager's door open, he took the paper out of the waste-paper basket and stuffed it into his pocket.

He argued with himself all the way downstairs: the manager must know already. True. But he must not know that the clerks take advantage of me. 'Discipline,' he heard the manager saying, leaning across his desk, 'we must have discipline in the office, Drover,' and Conrad, his lips dry with despair, knowing that he was about to be given a month's notice, heard with astonishment and disbelief, 'It's because I think you will be able to keep a firm hand on the clerks that I'm appointing you to <u>Chine's</u> position. You are young, Drover,' and the manager had sucked his teeth and smiled. 'There's nothing a young man can't do, given energy, given ambition.'

Conrad was taken by surprise. All his life he had been taken by surprise. People had promoted him when he had expected dismissal; they had praised him when he had expected blame. One day, he knew, they would find out. The director's nephew was the first.

Nobody had taken his seat. He hardly had time to raise the menu in front of his thin melancholy irritable face before the proprietress had flung herself towards his table. He was astonished every day at her promptitude. Old enough to be his mother, in a striped jumper to match her tea-room, she moved, as he sat down, as quickly and securely between the orange and blue art china, between the small tables with their check cloths, like a cat.

'Yes?' she breathed anxiously. 'Yes?' and whistled with nerves down the back of his neck.

'The lunch,' he said. The *à la carte* menu was a façade of respectability. It contained nothing that was not already included in the lunch, each course marked a little more expensively.

'The tomato soup,' he said. 'The steak and kidney pie.'

'I'm sorry. The pie's finished.'

'I always have pie. You might have known. You might have kept – '

'I thought perhaps you weren't coming in.'

'I always come in. I'll have a cutlet. And the fruit salad.' He realized that the menu was shaking in his hand; the coloured figures in crinolines under 'The Sign of the Mulberry Tree' wavered. 'Please,' he said, 'I believe today I'd like you to send out for a glass of stout.'

'I must ask you for the money, I'm afraid.' He could hardly hear what she said, and he told her to repeat it, nervously and irritably; he never realized that she was more afraid of him and his chief clerk's voice than of any other customer. She had always assumed that he was a Civil Servant burdened with secrets and responsibilities. 'A stout,' she said archly to her assistant, 'for our Slavedriver,' and felt a thrill of pride when the bottle was carried in. It made the whole restaurant more masculine. 'I think I shall change the name to the "Cocoa Tree",' she confided to Conrad, putting down the bottle beside him.

He did not answer. He was thinking how Milly had said, 'You'd be no use with a gun.' What on earth had made her say that? He had no use for a gun. The remark worried him. He was thinking of it when he got up, paid his bill, and left the tea-room. His face was intent, full of secrecy and care, he held himself badly; no one could have told what an absurd sentence he was repeating silently. Outside he raised his hand a little way and held it stiffly. For about two seconds it was still; long enough for a shot. But what on earth would he want to shoot at? A succession of faces flickered before him: the manager, the director's nephew, a succession of clerks, a plump man laughing outside the Berkeley, a lined yellow face smiling, his own features reflected in plate-glass. I should never have the nerve to do anything like that, he thought; shooting doesn't do any good. A girl ran past him towards a bus stop: she was laughing to herself and there was a smut on her cheek. He became suddenly conscious that complete happiness had brushed his coat, had nearly knocked the umbrella from his arm. He looked after her, but she was already out of sight, a piece of scarlet material vanishing into the interior of a moving bus.

A flower shop filled the air with scent.

Shooting doesn't do any good. All one wants is a little confidence, a belief in God, a flower in the buttonhole, music from a carillon, from mid-air, 'energy and ambition, Drover', love, a theatre ticket, love. With decision he stepped into the shop. 'A dozen of those saffron roses. How much are they?' The price staggered him, but he took them; it was too late, he had asked for them, and in any case, music from a carillon, love, extravagance, a piece of scarlet material disappearing.

When he was half a mile away he saw they had given him pink roses.

He swung his hand to throw them in the gutter; he was furious and disappointed: but an old lady stared at him in amazement, and he lowered his hand. He pretended that he had been signalling to a friend, smiled and nodded, and turned to a shop window: it was a gun shop. Two long double-barrelled guns were hung above a stuffed pheasant in a glass case. The coincidence astonished him. He heard Milly again make a light and meaningless remark, 'You'd be no use with a gun', and through his own transparent image, through the umbrella and the bouquet of flowers and the attaché case, he saw a row of small metal objects; the many-sided chambers caught the light like steel dice. The roar of buses sounded louder as the carillon ceased to play in the high tower of Atkinson's.

A little confidence, a belief in God. The manager, the director's nephew, myself. Conrad was happy, smiling into the barred window. 'Discipline, Drover, discipline,' and suppose that the retort was a raised revolver. 'I much regret . . . a month's notice,' the plump face staring at the plump hands on the mahogany desk, expecting a man to take dismissal in a sporting spirit, to go without complaint to the streets to the dole (but there was no dole for a professional man). Suppose instead, when that moment came, as that moment certainly would come one day, suppose instead one simply raised a hand and fired. Would the face have time to show astonishment?

'You would be a murderer.'

But I've seen through that; you can't shame me any longer with a word like murderer; I know what a murderer is – Jim is a murderer. The law has told me that, impressed it on me through three long days, counsel have made expensive speeches on the point; six shopkeepers, three Civil Servants, two doctors, and a well-known co-respondent have discussed it together and come to that conclusion – Jim is a murderer, a murderer is Jim. Why shouldn't I be a murderer myself? Always, from the time I went to school, I have wanted to be like Jim. It's no good calling me a murderer. I've seen through that.

Of course, he said to himself, I'm joking. But why shouldn't the joke go a little further? I'll go into the shop and think all the time, when I've bought what I'm going to buy, I shall never be afraid of anyone again. Of course, when the shopman asks me what I want, I'll make some excuse, the joke will be over, there'll be nothing more to laugh about then, I'll go out of the shop and catch a bus.

'Oh, yes, sir,' the shopkeeper was saying. 'This is the very type Lord Blendowe was using last autumn. He was pleased, very pleased with it. Feel the balance, sir. Of course it's not a gun for every occasion.' Conrad Drover watched them from the doorway, the bouquet of roses hung down to the pavement. 'It's a *sporting* gun, sir. When the birds are coming over well and high . . .'

111

They bent over the gun, they sighted it, they smoothed it with their fingers. The shopman became confidential. 'Is it true, sir, I have heard it remarked, that Mr Jones had not rented a moor this year? No, not Mr Fred Jones. He's shooting with Lord Taveril. Mr 'Gee-Gee' Jones, sir.'

Conrad entered the shop. He was smiling. He laid the roses on the counter and sat down. Nobody paid him any attention. 'No, not many Americans this year, sir. We can't say that we're sorry. We have few American customers. They bring their own guns across with them. Machine-guns it will be before long. We hear a good many stories of their conduct, as you might expect, sir. They're not sportsmen, sir, they're killers.'

Conrad got up again and began to walk round the shop. There was a thick carpet on the floor. His feet sank in the blue and scarlet pile, and one of his roses, a little overblown, shed its petals where he walked. In all the glass cases were arms: double-barrelled guns, rifles, revolvers.

The shopman tittered. 'Oh, yes, I had heard that, sir. That was Lord Taveril's shoot, was it not? Shot the beater in the leg. His lordship is often in here, sir. He told us about it himself.'

Conrad said suddenly in his chief clerk's voice, 'Is nobody going to attend to me?' The shopman looked at him, raised his eyebrows, called 'Mr Fanshawe, forward', and continued his story. Mr Fanshawe appeared behind the counter. He had grey hair and wore a morning coat. The sale of weapons seemed to require morning coats, deep carpets, and polish everywhere – polish on the mahogany cases, on shoes, on hair and on nails.

'I wanted to buy a revolver,' Conrad said.

'Certainly, sir, single action, double action. What are you contemplating?' He drew out a case and began to press revolvers on Conrad. 'The advantage of this new type of safety catch, sir. . . . A little heavy perhaps, this . . . this is a beautiful little instrument, sir, perhaps the most beautiful we have ever stocked. A lady's model, but perfectly reliable over any distance up to fifty feet.' Suddenly Conrad thought that the joke had gone far enough; he did not want a revolver; his hand was trembling again. He said: 'I'll think it over.'

Another identical grey object weighed down his hand and against his own will his fingers tightened: I shall be afraid of no one ever again: the drums of his ears beat 'discipline, Drover, discipline', 'a pram on a taxi'. He almost shouted at the assistant, 'But I have no licence.'

'Of course, sir, you have to produce the licence at the time of sale. If you were a regular customer we might waive a point, but naturally you will understand, sir, that we could not take the responsibility with a stranger.' He was breaking it gently; he was under the impression that Conrad might be disappointed at not being allowed to leave the shop with a beautiful instrument capable of killing a man with reliability over a distance of not more than fifty feet. 'No,' Conrad said with pleasure, very glad that his joke was over, 'I have no licence.'

'Perhaps I could interest you in a householder's air pistol. No licence required.' The man's voice was perfunctory. The pomp of carpet and morning coat and glittering mahogany was not required for the sale of an air pistol.

'No, no, I must see about the licence, and then I'll return.'

'You have left your flowers on the counter,' icily.

'Thank you.'

Mr Fanshawe had already turned his back. Conrad went out scattering rose petals. A bus went by, but no one pursued it, no one with complete happiness in her face ran past him to disappear, a scrap of scarlet material. The joke had not been very funny, hardly worth telling to Milly, hardly likely to make them both forget for a while Jim in prison,

Thursday's execution, and laugh. For the first time in his life he was touched by hatred of his brother. How long before one could smile or laugh? How long these cramped muscles of the mouth? How long the awareness that a moment's merriment was treacherous? The palm of his hand was still cold and weighted with gun metal.

The thought occurred to him a little later: suppose Milly has succeeded, suppose Mrs Coney has signed; suppose Jim is reprieved. The idea weighed as heavily on his mind as the revolver in his palm; the weight of eighteen years descended on him. Would even Jim want that? But it was their duty to assume that life, simply life as an abstraction, without pleasure or hope or change, was what Jim would prefer to death. If Jim died they would be marked for a long time with horror; but they would live nevertheless. There would be consolations in time; they would be able to talk naturally together; some sort of a life might be painfully constructed. But if Jim lived, they would be condemned to a kind of death themselves. The end of the eighteen years would be always in their sight, chilling any chance merriment, the flat end to every story. Jim put his mouth against the wire netting and said, 'It would be a good job if Milly married again.'

In his attaché case Conrad carried a pair of pyjamas, a sponge-bag, slippers, and a few papers. He opened it in the kitchen and packed away the contents neatly in corners; Milly had not come home. He boiled the kettle and listened, washed his hands and listened; upstairs the broken front-door banged back and forth. He wondered what was keeping her, put the flowers in water; the shop had given him its poorest flowers and one rose had already shed its petals. Presently he went upstairs.

He opened the door of Milly's room. He did not need Jim's photograph on a table by the bed to tell him that it was her room. He knew her scent: pretty and cheap. It had blown on him down passages: across the room where the shorthand typists sat; out of shop doors in Oxford Street; next him at the cinema. But it did not occur to him that the scent was a very common one, but that Milly was very often in his thoughts. He was never safe from her intrusion, for when the free samples of 'Nuit d'Amour' were exhausted, all the thousands of coupons in the women's pages filled up, and the scent was changed ('Vrai Paris' seeping through his door at the office, in and out of lifts and on the moving staircase), it was still the thought and image of Milly that he noticed, for Milly's scent too had changed. She was not bold and experimental like Kay; she could not afford to be, filling up innumerable forms, receiving the casket the size of a matchbox which had been pictured across half a page of *Modern*, the tiny pot of rouge, the tiny tube of cream, scent in a bottle that might have come from a doll's house.

He glanced at the table. Even now there was a form half filled in. 'I declare that I have not made a previous application. . . .' She had signed her name, but had not yet written her address. 'Milly Drover,' the spidery writing fell apart between the letters, which ended in a jagged hole and a blot of ink. The writing seemed to him, after the copper-plate of the office, very individual; she had been absent-minded, paused and hurried on, ended fiercely because of her thoughts. He felt tender towards her writing, touching it with his finger, wondering how long it was since the ink had dried. 'Milly Drover,' he read again; it pleased him that their names were the same; for a moment it seemed that she was his wife. He took out his fountain pen and added his address in rough imitation of her writing. When he looked up again he saw her image in the mirror watching him.

'What are you doing, Conrad?'

'He read out, "I declare that I have not made a previous application. Signed Milly Drover. Address, 16, Wallace Road.'

'Wallace Road,' she said vaguely, and then began to

115

laugh. 'Conrad, what a fool you are. I'm so happy.'

'Happy?' he asked incredulously. There was a slight flush on her cheek-bones, and her wide mouth trembled; it occurred to him that she had been drinking.

'Yes. Everything's going to be all right. I feel it. I made her sign. She didn't want to sign, but I made her sign. I feel – I feel as if there's nothing I can't do.' She took off her hat and threw it on the bed. Conrad had never known her talk so much; he was anxious, startled, disappointed. He was like a man who had been separated from one he loved for many years and returned to find her almost unrecognizable, so drastically had time worked on her. 'I've never tried before,' she said, 'to make people do things. Jim was always here. I didn't know that I could, but I can.' She came and sat on the edge of the dressing-table beside him and stretched her arms and yawned.

'You've had something to drink, haven't you?' he asked uneasily.

'Yes, Conrad, three sherries. Just like that. One after the other.' She was laughing at him; that, he thought ruefully, was what remained of the familiar Milly. Yesterday she had taken him seriously, she had appealed to him; the mood had not lasted.

'Where did you get the money?'

'Mr Conder treated me.'

'Who's Conder?' he asked sharply. 'I've never heard of Conder.'

'I hadn't this morning, but he's helping me. He's a journalist. He knows Kay. Don't be so gloomy. Look at yourself in the glass.'

'I've never known you talk so much. He's a clever man to make you talk.'

She pulled his tie out of his coat. 'He's middle-aged. Conrad, and bald and married with six children. You needn't be jealous.'

116

'Jealous,' he said, 'that's a curious word to use to me. Jealous?'

'I didn't mean anything odd,' she said. His sharpness had sobered her; she spoke in a low voice, defensively; it was the familiar Milly who spoke in that way; even if he had closed his eyes or turned his back, he would have known how she was looking, away from him, into corners, shifting her gaze, not from guile but from fear that almost anywhere she might find an enemy. He remembered her in the cramped smoky church, on the day of her wedding, amid the smell of anthracite and the drumming from the distant drills in the High Street, answering 'Yes' with sudden loud defiance as if even in the church she expected enemies and foresaw unhappiness.

'I brought you some flowers,' he said. 'I put them in water.'

'I saw them. They're lovely.'

'They aren't much. They gave me the wrong ones. And they're overblown. They won't last long,' and immediately he thought of Thursday.

She said with less conviction: 'Everything's going to be all right. I feel it.'

'You mustn't expect too much from that petition.'

'I made her sign.'

'At the best it means eighteen years.'

'He'll be alive,' she said stubbornly. 'He'll be glad to be alive.'

'And you?'

She looked at him almost with horror. 'Me? Of course I'll be glad. It will be heaven. I'll be seeing him.'

'Once a month.'

'What are you getting at? Do you want him to hang?'

Conrad walked away from the mirror, along the bed, ten feet to the end wall, and back again, touched the mirror and made it swing, throwing up the reflection of his own face and the bed behind towards the ceiling. 'I'm not sure. I'm seeing things clearer.'

'You needn't stay here,' Milly said, 'if you want him to hang. You can go to hell.'

'You're more important than he is.'

'Who to? You?'

'Yes. What's the good of pretending? When I say you're pretty, I mean pretty to me. When I say important, I mean to me, not to Ramsay MacDonald, not to the Queen.'

She said quickly, trying to divert him: 'I saw the Queen just now. Going into a cinema. Why does she wear hats like that?'

He took no notice. 'Can't we ever enjoy ourselves again because Jim's made a fool of himself?'

'I thought you were fond of him.'

'I am fond of him. But he's making me hate him. I've got to hate somebody for this. Something's wrong, and the constable's dead, and I can't hate the law.'

She said with despair: 'Be reasonable. It's nobody's fault. Hating doesn't get you anywhere, any more than loving does. A bed in a hospital, that's about where both get you. You look too far ahead, and you spoil everything. I was happy enough when I came home. I'd done something. I felt sure we'd save Jim, but you talk and talk and now all I want to do is to go to bed and cry.'

He looked at her with astonishment. 'That's odd, because I was cheerful too. Till you came in. I had a joke to tell you. I went into one of those Bond Street shops where they sell guns and pretended I wanted a revolver.'

'Why a revolver?'

'It was for a joke. I ordered the shopman about. Complained. Then I said I hadn't got a licence and came away. It seemed a good joke at the time.'

'It's the flattest joke,' Milly said, 'that I've ever heard.'

'It does seem flat now,' he said wonderingly, and they

both at the same moment began to laugh. He did not know why, but as he set the mirror swinging for the second time and saw bed and face and powder-bowls rocket out of sight, he was back in the mood of carillons ringing out the hour in Atkinson's, of flower scent above the pavement, and of the girl running past knocking his umbrella aside. His face was no longer stiff with suspicion of unspoken criticisms. She had told him that he was a fool and that his joke was flat and that he could go to hell. He cherished her words as if they had been the highest praise, lost his suspicion with the idea that perhaps she had said the worst she could of him.

'And this,' he said, 'this is flat enough: "I declare I have not made" . . .'

'No,' she said, 'that's not flat, that's funny,' with tears in her eyes. 'Conrad, you fool. You fool, Conrad.'

The mood carried them safely over several hours. Kay had not returned at tea-time; by supper he already felt that he had lived for several years with Milly. But the dark and the turning on of the light drove them a little way apart. 'It won't be long before it's winter,' he said. 'Is Kay all right?'

'She knows what's what,' Milly said. She lit the gas and drew in her chair and began to crochet; he watched her for a while. She rushed at it with a reckless disregard of her pattern; again and again she had to unpick a row. The result was a patch of striped material neither round nor oval. Conrad took out his papers and tried to work, but her nearness confused him. Her legs were crossed; their thinness, her bony knee, the tangle of her moving fingers, the red slippers trodden down at the heels which dangled from her toes, her bent head, the high cheek-bones, filled him with a sadness he did not try to explain. Painfully, loop by loop, she unpicked; recklessly she dashed at the row again, the pattern fell from her knee and its corner was singed by the heat of the flame. The cold burning light scorched him where he sat; he turned

119

the fire lower, and her face darkened as the glow retreated. Her legs reminded him of the limbs of native children photographed by missionaries. The children stared back at him from white screens in the county school, wide-eyed, uncomprehending, with no idea of the pathos they were intended to convey. A bony knee, a slipper trodden at the heel, they were enough to rouse again his longing to hate, Jim, the director's nephew, the man joking outside the Berkeley, anyone who threatened in however indirect a manner that bony knee, that slipper trodden down.

'What is it?' he said. 'What are you making?'

She raised her work against the light. 'Something's gone wrong,' she said. 'It oughtn't to be nearly square.'

'What is it?'

'A béret.'

'Doesn't the pattern help?'

'The pattern,' she said. 'Oh, the pattern. No one can understand the pattern.' She began to read very rapidly: '3 treble in the 5th chain from the hook, miss 2 chain, 1 double crochet in the next, what do you call it – asterisk – miss 2 chain, 4 treble in the next, miss 2 chain –'

'Give it to me,' Conrad said. 'I'll show you.'

'You can't – you can't crochet?'

'It's easier than book-keeping,' Conrad said.

'You know,' Milly said, 'what's wrong with you is that you're too perfect – you're quiet, you're clever, you can crochet. What could a wife do with you?' She mocked him in a voice completely empty of amusement; she had caught his own mood; he stared at her with a sadness and a hunger which was hardly sensual at all. It was a hunger to release her; she had no more business here than the dumb sun-scorched children in the stove-heated county schoolroom. A memory which had inhabited a corner of the room, which had made a third to their talk, fled and left them aware of how they were alone together. Other occasions of partial loneliness came back to him, days when Jim was at work and Milly had consented to be with him, slightly tearful, slightly satirical at the cinema, on the bus top grinding down Hammersmith Broadway towards Chiswick, pulling at the window beside her to open it, in Kew Gardens pretending to understand the names written on the steel labels, tired and quiet and wanting her tea in the tropical heat of the Palm House. But they had never been so alone as between the gas stove and the gas fire, on either side the porcelain-topped table.

'I'm tired,' she said, 'I'm going to go to bed. Kay won't be in for hours yet if she's with a man.' She took a quick suspicious look at him as if she were wondering: Are you a man? You are quiet, you are clever, you can crochet. Are you a man?

'I'll make up a bed on these chairs if you'll show me where your blankets are.' She opened a cupboard door. 'They've never been used,' she said. 'Somebody gave them us for a wedding present,' and he was aware again of the hot church and the distant drills. 'How jealous you were of me,' she said. 'I laughed at you with Jim. He didn't like it. You were scowling when I came up the church.'

'Did you notice me?' he said. 'But I wasn't scowling. I didn't feel like that at all.'

She buried her hands in the deep warm pile of blankets. 'How did you feel?' She was rushing him as she had rushed her crochet, recklessly.

'Oh,' he said, 'I loved you even then.'

Then she was painfully, loop by loop, unpicking. 'Well, it's only right for a brother.'

'Give me the blankets.' He began to make his bed and did not look up when she said, 'Good night, Conrad,' and went upstairs to bed. Of course, he thought, she wasn't leading me on; she was just careless as she is when she's working. She can't think of me as a man. Conrad. It was the name, he

121

could almost believe, that prevented it. His parents had no business calling him by such a name, the name of a seaman, a merchant officer who once lodged in their house. 'What was there about him?' he had often asked. 'Why call me after him? Was he clever?' 'Not that I know of,' they said. 'Was he kind to you?' 'Not particularly.' 'What happened to him?' 'I dunno.' 'Was he with you long?' 'A few months.' 'Then why, why?' 'I dunno. Gave us the idea, I suppose. No good calling you Herbert. Your uncle was broke.' So 'Conrad, Conrad, Conrad' had been flicked at him across the desks, across the asphalt yard, driving him into isolation, while the Jims, the Herberts, the Henrys flocked together and shared secrets. So 'Good night, Conrad,' leaving him alone in the kitchen. So happiness running by him. So the wrong roses dropping on the pavement. His umbrella that leant in a corner slipped and rattled on the floor, and at the same moment he heard a door open in the hall above. It was Kay, of course, though at first he hardly recognized her steps. They were light and slow and lingering. Standing there beside the chair with a blanket over his arm, he could almost imagine that he was listening to a rich woman, walking over a deep carpet, thoughtful and sensual, waiting for a lover. She came down the stairs and he waited for her enviously. She was humming a tune, she was happy, she had got what she wanted.

I'm right, he thought when he saw her face. She had more colour than usual – that meant nothing, for she put it on herself, but her face glowed with health. She looked sleepy and satisfied like a cat after milk.

'Milly gone to bed?'

'Yes.' She yawned and stretched and kicked a piece of paper across the floor. He knew that she had not come into the kitchen alone; she had brought a man with her; he was in every sleek movement, he was in every thought; he was all but in her body still. 'Where've you been?'

'Enjoying myself,' she said. She looked at the clock and he saw her as if she were rising reluctantly from a bed. 'I'd better be off.' She was remembering the factory, the rattle of the boxes and the clangour of the machines.

'Tomorrow's Sunday.'

'So it is. Tomorrow,' she caressed the word and watched him with malicious amusement. He knew that she wanted him to ask her questions and he would have disappointed her if he could. He put two chairs together and arranged a sheet and two blankets. 'What a housewife,' she said.

'Why don't you go to bed?'

'Do you grudge a girl a little fun?'

'What do you mean?'

'You'd do it yourself if you could,' she said. 'It makes a girl tired all the same, but thank God for men.' Then she trailed up the stairs and he heard her open Milly's door and begin to talk. She'll turn her out, he thought, she won't stand for that; one might as well have a tart in the house, and he listened for angry voices, for slamming doors. But he heard nothing but Kay's voice talking on. She's stopping her ears, he thought, and then – she'll be half undressed, she'll catch cold, and again with sorrow and hunger he thought of the desperate eyes and the smell of anthracite, of bony knees and trodden heels and half-starved native children on a white screen. 'Oh, my God,' he said aloud, 'this is too much; it's not fair.' He meant that it was not fair, the thought that if his brother were hanged, Milly might be desperate enough to marry him.

He put down the blankets and went to the foot of the stairs, then mounted step by step. He heard Kay talking, Milly was silent. 'Three months, darling, since the last. I was just ready for anything.' The door was open, and he could see Kay sitting on the bed; Milly had her back turned to him; she was crouched on a stool at her dressing-table brushing her hair. She had taken off her stockings and he saw how the skin of her legs was a little rubbed and abraded; he could see the gleam of the thin hair. Her eyes were looking back from the glass at Kay, while the hand brushed and brushed. She was tired and anxious and at the mercy of anyone at all. She's too tired, he thought, to tell her to go.

'Darling, such a bed. But it took ages to bring him to the point. How he talked. He told me all about his wife.'

'His wife?' Milly whispered.

'She's dead. But he *would* tell me what a wonderful marriage it had been. And afterwards he sat up in bed and began talking about her again. She painted pictures. He said they were wonderful. He said, "Do you like pictures?" and I said I liked pictures of dogs and people bathing. So he said, "You're academic," and I told him that he couldn't call me names just because he'd had what he wanted. And then I got up and dressed; and he called a taxi and we said we'd meet tomorrow. And that was all.'

Milly said, 'What are you going to do tomorrow?'

'The same again, I expect,' Kay said. 'A girl's got to work off steam.' She leant back on the bed and stretched her legs. 'It's rotten for you, Milly,' she said. 'You haven't had a man for months. It's not healthy.'

'I couldn't do it,' Milly said, 'not with a stranger.' She swung away from the mirror and said to Kay in a low, savage, curiously innocent voice. 'What does it feel like with a stranger?'

'A pig in a poke,' Kay said. 'Sometimes you hit on someone wonderful. Sometimes it's not worth the trouble of untying your shoes.'

'And tonight?' Milly asked in a dry cracked childish voice.

'Oh, it wasn't bad,' Kay said, 'if he hadn't talked so much. There's someone I'd have liked better, but you can't always have what you want. When you've got a pash for someone like I have, anybody's better than nothing; it makes you so that you can't wait. Anyway, he gave me a lovely supper, and oh, Milly, I forgot to tell you the best part of it all – the Mouse. It came out as bold as you please. He threw a shoe at it. Fancy my nearly forgetting to tell you about the Mouse.'

How simple she seemed to make it, Conrad thought, retreating a few steps down the stairs as Kay crossed from Milly's room to her own, how simple this going to bed. It was only love which complicated the act. He heard the door of Kay's room close behind her satisfied, sleepy and triumphant figure, and again he came hesitatingly up the stairs and saw Milly in front of her mirror with her thin knees drawn up nearly to her chin. He watched her, tried to think of her savagely without her clothes as one thought of an expensive prostitute in a restaurant, but the thin legs, the hopeless immaturity of her breasts failed to excite him. Kay had excited him more than this, with the smell of a man still about her. Why don't I go to bed then, he wondered; why stay and stare at a half-naked girl unless I want her? He told himself that he would be satisfied to hold her all night in his arms and talk, do nothing but talk, talk of what they could do to help the man they both loved. He was without jealousy or passion, but when he heard her say, 'Conrad, come in,' and saw that she had seen him all the while in the glass, he felt ashamed as if she were a girl he had got into trouble.

And he had brought trouble on her. This was not happiness brushing his umbrella, not love watching him at second-hand, from the mirror. 'Shut the door.' She whispered the words. She was full of shame and fear and unhappiness. Her skin was as dry as a child's with fever. She was a child who had been aged suddenly by sickness. He remembered a boy at school who had died from influenza, how in the last hours before the nurses had put a screen round the bed, he had watched all that went on in the sickroom with a fallacious, an elderly wisdom; he was not

125

really wise, not really old; he was only feverish and very weak.

'Did you hear what she said?' Milly asked, 'that it was rotten for me? Did you hear what she'd been doing?' If he had felt the slightest lust, he would have fled; it was the unexcitement in his love, the element of pity, that kept him there. It seemed unbearable to him that she should suffer.

'You ought to turn her out of the house.'

'Conrad,' she said, 'don't be a fool. Don't be a fool, Conrad. She's right. Eighteen years. Do you think I could stand it? One's got to begin some time.' He wanted to tell her that this was sick-room wisdom, but there was no time to argue. She was speaking to him and he wanted to stop her. Otherwise she would suffer later at having been the one to ask, and she had already enough suffering to bear; he wanted to spare her anything he could. 'I want – ' she said, and even then, in his hurry to interrupt, he noted with pain and without surprise that she was too honest to use a kindlier or more tender word.

'Listen,' he said quietly, 'you know I love you. Let me stay. That was why I came upstairs. I couldn't sleep.' He felt no guilt at all; this did not harm his brother, this hopeless attempt to shield her, for she had not even been deceived; she was glad, she was grateful, she was his friend, but she didn't believe a word he said. Then she touched him with timidity, and his flesh stirred, and he felt a degree of guilt which only the bed and the tiring of his body and the forgetting of his love in the direct contact of skin with skin, the thrust of lust, could temporarily and in part assuage. When he felt her shudder, he had a dull sense of an irrevocable injury which one of them had done to the other. Love had been close to him, in the kitchen, before the glow and the hum of the gas, between chair and chair, which had escaped him now in the bed, in the dark. One of them had injured the other, but it was not their fault. They had been driven to it, and holding

126

her body close to him with painful tenderness, it was hate he chiefly felt, hate of Jim, of a director's nephew, of two men laughing in Piccadilly. When he awoke in the night she was crying, and nothing that he could do would stop her tears. He thought of Kay happily asleep in the next room and lust, he thought, they call that lust and this is love. He meant the hate and the pain and the sense of guilt and the sound of crying in the greying room and sleeplessness and the walls shaking as the early morning lorries drove out of London.

*

'Caroline,' the voice said, 'Caroline.' It added with metallic kindliness. 'It's not like you to forget a friend. Ten years ago . . .' The Assistant Commissioner plodded back through those years; they led through suffering, through home-sickness, through resignation; along jungle paths, across mosquito-haunted nights, past a good many deaths of one sort or another. But the telephone did not allow much time for reflection. 'I want you to dine with me – on Monday.'

He had just time to emerge, as it were backwards, at the other end of ten years; the final dinner at the Army and Navy to the only man with whom he cared to spend his last hours in England; his valet waving decorously from the quay; the mist which hid the Needles, hid England altogether, so that he could not give the final glance which sentiment would conventionally have compelled from him. Before that – of course Caroline telling him to write, pouring out tea, turning to a politician.

'I really don't think . . .' His table was littered with papers; the wireless invention was not satisfactory; the unofficial reports on Drover were coming in from various districts.

'You can't refuse me. It's absurd. The day after tomorrow. Only two hours.'

'If you could – er – see my, my desk.'

127

'Such old friends. We mustn't allow the threads to be dropped. Too absurd. After ten years.' The appeal to sentiment was heartlessly efficient; it had struck him in the place where he was most vulnerable and at the hour when he was most alone. Even his secretary had left him in his room at the Yard; all those men, whose hours of duty corresponded with his, were departing; their voices faded down the long passages between the glass cubicles.

'When I'm a bit, a bit clearer. I've got a lot to learn here. Different methods, Caroline. I'm really busy.'

The voice said, 'But I want you particularly.' It hesitated. 'I'm going abroad next week. I don't know when I shall be back.' He was quite sure that she was lying; but there were very few people who lied to get his company. The men on night duty were arriving; he heard them walking softly by his door; he could see the shadows through the ground glass. He knew that they resented his presence. They believed that he was prying into the affairs of their departments, interfering. When he first came, he explained several times as clearly as his inarticulate tongue would permit that he wanted to understand how each department worked, not in order to criticize but in order himself to pull his weight. They had never made the least pretence of believing him. He had tried to convince them; against his conscience he had sometimes refrained from criticism when criticism was required; they merely concluded that he was saving up for some grand devastating report to the Home Secretary.

'Thank you very much then. I'll come, but I shall have to, have to hurry away.' He rang off, and the sudden cessation of that harsh but friendly voice made him feel his isolation acutely. The room all round him was dark; only his desk was lit by the green-shaded lamp. Somewhere a long way off a telephone bell rang and a voice could be heard speaking, but through the glass door the long passage was now in complete darkness. He was like a general left alone at headquarters to study the reports from every unit; they littered his desk. But he was not sheltered in a château behind miles of torn country; the front line was only a hundred yards away, where the trams screamed down the Embankment and the buses circled Trafalgar Square.

It was hard, he thought, to get any clear idea of a war carried on in this piecemeal way throughout a city. He was not used yet to visualizing a situation from a policeman's colourless report; he had been accustomed in the East to seeing with his own eyes the casualties of law: the stabbed soldier, the smouldering hut, the body hanging from a branch.

'No references were made to the Drover case at the Labour demonstrations at . . .'

'A collection in aid of Mrs Drover was made at the strike headquarters at . . .'

'A proposal to hold a demonstration against Drover's sentence in Trafalgar Square tomorrow was vetoed by headquarters, who have expressed their willingness to meet the employers on the subject of short-time rates . . .'

'It is generally assumed here that a reprieve will be granted. Five thousand people have signed the petition.'

'Some indignation . . .'

'Generally apathetic . . .'

'Pronounced feeling against members of the Force . . .'

'No particular interest . . .'

With some impatience he pushed these reports on one side and turned to the Streatham papers; here was something about which it was possible to feel, I am fighting for what is right. In the case of Drover he was upholding a system in which he had no interest because he was paid to uphold it: he was a mercenary, and a mercenary soldier could not encourage himself with the catchwords of patriotism – my country right or wrong; self-determination of peoples; justice. He fought because he was paid to fight, and only occasionally did the sight of some brutality lend conviction to the brain with which he fought. At other times the highest motive he could offer was that of doing his job; there were no abstract reasons to compel him to forbid this meeting, to break up that, to have this Socialist arrested for seditious speaking, to guard that Fascist's platform while he spoke in terms of bayonets and machine guns; it was the will of the organization he served. It was only when he was tired or depressed or felt his age that he dreamed of an organization which he could serve for higher reasons than pay, an organization which would enlist his fidelity because of its inherent justice, its fair distribution of reward, its reasonableness. Then he told himself with bitterness that he was too old to live so long. His thin face, yellowed by more fevers than he could count, lined by the years of faithful mercenary service, would grow for a moment envious at the thought of younger men who might live to serve something which they believed worthy of their service.

4

'MARGARET,' Mr Surrogate said, and turned his hand palm upwards on the sheet, 'Margaret.' His voice fell, his words became inaudible, and Davis laid a towel across the hot-water can and hesitated by the window. Should he draw up the blind and let in the sunlight? In Woburn Square the children were yelping on the pavement and the man with the Sunday papers called to the taximen on the rank.

'Good food,' Mr Surrogate said suddenly, still with that explanatory and reasonable palm outspread. Davis decided: let him sleep, let the bastard sleep: and tiptoed respectfully out, a gentleman's gentleman.

The sands were pink of an evening, the sea silver. At the rippled edge, far across the pink sands, the sea-birds sat, small and white and upright, like unlit candles. Margaret stood and stared and would not come in to dinner. 'Good food wasted,' Mr Surrogate said, pecking at her elbow like a hungry bird. 'Oh, go to hell,' and she was Kay leaning away from him towards the bed. Mr Surrogate woke and sat up and faced Margaret Surrogate's cold appraisal from the wall. 'I married the artist in her,' he explained to the reporter at the funeral; he was prepared; had expected several journalists; hid his disappointment with difficulty from the single inexperienced boy from a news agency. 'She was always, to me, more than a woman.' The boy stared at him and blew his nose: he had a streaming cold.

It's true, Mr Surrogate said, not aloud, for Davis was in the next room, you were more than a woman. I wasn't worthy of you. He was daunted by the canvases which now decorated Caroline Bury's wall, daunted by the brief uncomfortable sexual passion in which Margaret had been the leader, leaving him worn out, humiliated, with the knowledge of her dissatisfaction. More than a woman. Kay was a woman, leaning back towards the bed, calling out, 'No, Mr Surrogate, no. Please not,' afterwards on the pillows whispering into his ear how bad he was, how strong.

I've betrayed you again, Mr Surrogate said humbly to the face. Man is a beast, a lecherous beast. He may mate above him, but presently he finds his proper level. Nasty, brutish, short, that was how Hobbes described a man's life. Mr Surrogate patted the grey hair above his ears, squinting sideways at the mirror. One ran through life quickly: the Fabian Society, hansoms at midnight, friendships with cultured plumbers, fighting for truth and justice, seeing violence prevail, lust prevail over the memory of love. Mr Surrogate's thoughts withdrew from that unhappy honeymoon in Cornwall. One grew old.

But Mr Surrogate's thoughts rose resiliently: one was not too old to conquer and satisfy a young and pretty woman. Things would have been different, he told himself, avoiding the photograph, if Margaret had been less artist, more woman, had been less cold; he stamped deep down the memory of that unsated passion. She never understood me.

'Davis, Davis,' he called, 'what's the time? My watch has stopped.'

'Half past nine, sir,' Davis called from the pantry. 'Will you take cereals or porridge, sir?'

'Cereals.' His complexion would not stand porridge too often. A small spot would appear on his nose. In four hours I shall have her here again. But he felt very little excitement. He even wondered whether he really wanted to see her again. He was not passionate; in middle age two days together with a girl were enough to exhaust him; after that passion had the same effect as porridge, a spot on the nose.

He stroked his skin gingerly; he was humble again before a mirror. It was odd that a young and pretty girl should fall for him. Of course there is my position. But the girl was stupid. She could never follow the reasoning of *No Compensation*. She wanted me to help her brother-in-law. But I had already spoken to Caroline; there was nothing more I could do. My bed, he thought, with a flash of intuition, she liked my bed, and he stared across the pink blankets, screwing up his lips histrionically at the thought that a bed might mean more to a girl than the authorship of *No Compensation*.

'Tea or coffee, sir?'

'Coffee, Davis.'

After all I am a public figure; I am the most advanced economic thinker in this country (a glance from those amused appraising eyes) and reluctantly he thought – I'm Margaret's husband – Margaret whose malicious vision lay in state in the picture galleries of every capital in Europe. A girl like that is not really fit for me. His ageing body, sated by its single indulgence, made not the least protest.

She may mean blackmail. The horrible thought occurred to him for the first time.

'Are you never going to bring breakfast, Davis?' he called irritably. I will not meet her. I'll lie in bed. I'm tired.

Oh, Margaret. Margaret. She was only twenty when she had married him; she had hardly begun to realize her power in paint. All those pictures, the three at the Tate, those on Caroline's walls, at Manchester, at Munich, in Berlin, belonged to him. 'To Mr W. H., the onlie begetter.' He was not proud of his inspiration. Those landscapes in which nature was so deftly, so wearily, so faintly caricatured meant nights of exhaustion, and the shrieking nerve. I've done you enough harm, Margaret. I'll be faithful. I'll give this girl up. He wanted to compel the portrait to believe him this time, that it was not the fear of blackmail which restrained him, that it was for her. I've only loved you, Margaret, he told her and thought a minute later: God knows, that *may* be true.

Davis brought in the breakfast tray and tactfully pushed under the bed with his foot a girl's hair slide.

'You've forgotten the soft sugar again, Davis.'

You dirty old bastard, you've been at it again, Davis thought, stepping on patent leather toes softly and quickly to the door.

*

'A nice little woman,' Conder said. He had breakfast in the café, rolls and coffee. It was not that he preferred a Continental breakfast or that he could not afford a larger one; he was well paid. But an accumulation of uneaten breakfasts was exchanged for holidays in Belgium, in France, in Switzerland, for pockets musical with foreign coins.

'You've forgotten the butter, Jules.'

'You've forgotten the sugar.'

'No knife, Jules.'

The young man ran back and forth from his counter with a lost look like a dog taken shopping. 'If only I could remember things. Even faces.'

Faces. Faces. Conder sat upright with a jerking neuralgic movement. I'd forgotten. I'm tired. I'm not myself. Milly's perplexed, suddenly flushed face (after three sherries), suddenly joyful (watching him scribble in a notebook), fled. He saw instead, behind Milly, Bennett watching him from a table near the door. 'What ought I to have done?' he asked Jules. 'He'd followed me. He must have followed me. The coincidence. Last night when I was talking to a friend, and again the night before that, after the meeting. He follows me everywhere. I haven't done him any harm.'

'You should be like me,' Jules said. 'I forget faces. You know, even Kay – I'm not clear what she looks like. My

134

mother – I remember a sort of chintz effect; she had huge breasts. My father – a moustache, a huge moustache. It seemed huge then. That's all I remember.'

Conder said: 'I'm afraid. I don't know what to do. Suppose he's in the street now, watching. I haven't done him any harm. But he may think I have, you see. I printed that story about the fight. And there's something else as well.'

'Does he know you?'

'I called on him once. Collecting for the Party. He may have an eye for faces. Like me. I have an eye for them.' They were like the portraits in an intimate picture gallery, hanging there always at the back of his mind: politicians, policemen, thieves; the man who drowned his wife at Shoreham, flushed and neat in the dock with a tiepin in the shape of a horse's head; the widow of the grocer who drew the Derby winner and who, dead drunk the same night, drove his car into the Thames, a widow with £20,000 of her own; she said, 'I've always been lucky at such things, raffles, I mean, and so on': Milly Drover. He could not keep her any longer in the centre of his attention, her portrait must be relegated to a gallery which was not often visited – perhaps a few years later a similarity of dress or scent would remind him ('a nice little woman'); he had an amazing memory for faces, for phrases, for stories of a startling kind. But now, for the moment, because he was tired, his memory was a jumble of pictures, a cacophony of sound. I've got to pull myself together. He poured out his coffee black.

Jules said: 'My memory. I've even forgotten that letter. I've been thinking of nothing but poor Drover.'

'Ought I to go to him,' Conder wondered, 'and explain?'

'Curious. It was from France. I don't know anyone in France except my father. And this was typed. Father would never have the money for a typewriter. I put it down for a moment and then you came in and there was the meeting,

135

and all yesterday there was this and that. I'll open it when I go up.'

'Come with me,' Conder said. 'He won't cut up rough if there are two of us. I can't stand all this watching and spying. I want to have it out with him. Oh, hell, Jules, you haven't given me a spoon.'

'What do you want a spoon for?' Jules said. 'Use your fingers. Listen. I've got to go to Mass, and then I want to see the priest about this petition. Don't you think it might help if a priest signed it? I must do something. I know how it'll be. Everyone'll get bored and just let it alone.'

'I've done what I can. I've got something else to think about now.'

'You see there's Kay's sister. I've got to do something.'

'Before you forget it like my spoon,' Condor said. 'Or that letter.'

'No, no. They're different. None of you are going to do as much for Drover as I am. I feel it. None of you are going to do as much.'

'Packet of "Weights",' a man said at the counter. 'I've bin standin' here while you talk long enough. I want a packet of "Weights". Unless I get a packet of "Weights" I'll break somethin'.'

'All right. All right,' Jules said.

Conder drank up his coffee and went out. The street was full of dogs and women and onion peel. The bells of one of the Soho churches were ringing. In the height of a pale-blue sky an aeroplane turned and twisted, leaving a trail of smoke which hung about for a time, then blew away. It was as if the pilot had begun an advertisement and then remembered it was Sunday. Men stood in their doorways and read the *News of the World* and spat. In Wardour Street and Shaftesbury Avenue they were reading the *Sunday Express*; in the almost empty Circus Conder bought an *Observer* and, sitting on a bus top, he read the editor's warning to Europe.

'War?' splashed a whole page. A book reviewer wrote: 'I am not in the habit of discovering masterpieces, but . . .'

'Camden Town,' Conder said. Mr MacDonald was going to fly back from Lossiemouth; there were to be several international conferences in agreeable cities in Southern Europe; a few thousand men had been knocked off the dole.

I won't be followed around, Conder thought. I won't be treated as he treated that treasurer. It's bad for my nerves. Indeed his nerves were in a shocking condition. Ever since he had rapped the skull of the wooden bear in Mrs Coney's passage he had lost control of the present and the past. Tentatively to Milly he had sketched in the children and the bath and the new house; all the familiar world was being snatched from him and sent tumbling over the Schaffhausen falls to be flung in spray against the coloured windows of a summer house. He clutched at a memory, but it was torn from him; even the tiepin in the shape of a horse's head whirled away on the rapids. 'Come with me,' he said to Jules, but Jules vanished. Milly's face blurred and disappeared. He who boasted a memory of faces could remember nothing but the features of one girl whose skirt he had clutched among the cuckoo clocks. What he remembered only too distinctly were despair, shame, tears. He had to remind himself that these were past. I need a holiday, he told himself. This is serious. It even occurred to him quite plainly for a moment that he had been too inventive; he had to draw the line immediately between what was real, Bennett following him, Bennett threatening him, and what was unreal, the child with whooping cough, the bath, again the past.

'Mr Bennett?' he said to the man on the ground floor. 'I want to see him. Is he in?' Dogs barked and bit each other in a zoological shop across the way, and very faintly, because the traffic was almost stilled, it was possible to hear the lions in Regent's Park roaring to be fed.

'There's nobody here called Bennett,' the man said. He

leant across the doorway and smoked a cigarette. 'Nice little dawgs,' he said. He was the kind of man, in his height and breadth and roughness, in the threat of his broken nose, who sells puppies in back streets.

Conder said, 'I know he lives here. On the top floor,' but he was beginning to doubt his memory.

'Take off your hat,' the man said. 'Take off your hat,' he repeated so fiercely, that Conder obeyed, raising his hat politely before the other's mutilated gaze.

'Bald,' the man said. 'Bald. I just guessed it was you. Come upstairs.'

Conder said, 'I wanted to apologize. In case he thought. ...' He clung to the drab street; a bus went by and in an upper window across the way a man was shaving. This was real, this he had to keep hold of. 'Come upstairs,' the man repeated, and Conder obeyed him, obeyed him because he had a loud voice and an assured manner, just as he had obeyed the elderly American reeking of eau-de-Cologne who had assured him that the Schaffhausen falls were something which no intelligent man should miss. So this mounting the dim staircase with fear loosening his bowels; so the long drive in the cold and an expensive tea and no pocket handkerchief and the girl laughing at him, while the pink and green falls went by.

'I only wanted to say – '

'Now look, just you look,' the man said and threw the door open.

'What at?' Conder asked. 'There's nothing.' A fire sank out of existence on the hearth; a table, a chair, a bed, but nothing else, not even a picture on the walls.

'Nothing,' the man said, 'he's gone, hopped it, and why? Left me with the room to let, hasn't paid his rent, hopped it, skedaddled, shot the moon. Have you a better name for it, and why?' The man advanced on Conder and Conder backed. 'And why? Because a mean, small, shabby rat who couldn't keep his finger out of other people's pies was following him around. His nerves couldn't stand it.' The big man's manner softened. 'Be reasonable. You don't need to have done much to get nerves. And how would you like to have been followed wherever you went by a mean, small, shabby rat with a bald head? I said to him, "Stick it out, the man doesn't know anything, he's just trying it on," and he promised he would. But when I got back last night that's what I found. Hopped. Skedaddled. Be reasonable,' the big man repeated. 'He's even took my pictures.'

'But,' Conder said, and he made the motion of pushing the stranger away with the palm of his hand, 'but I thought he was following *me*.' The other stared at him for a while and then began to laugh.

In the silent shabby street the sound was enough to wake the caged dogs, who behind the lowered shutters of the Sunday peace began again to bite and snarl and whine.

Conder cleared his throat and put his hand towards his bald head in an habitual gesture. It was comic, of course, it was comic. But islanded on one moment of the past, cabined above the rocking falls, he had the impression of all human contacts whirling from him in laughter, in fear, or simply (and he thought of Milly for almost the last time) in the press of other business.

*

Jules prayed, while the fat priest rose above the pulpit, and the congregation withered into attitudes of meekness, piety and inattention. He prayed with his face in his hands for Jim Drover. As his emotion welled out between his fingers, he felt the satisfaction of doing all he could for someone he had never seen; he was ready for incredible sacrifices, feeling a kinship with the crude Christ in plaster.

The priest addressed the congregation in French on the subject of sin; the word *péché, péché, péché,* held down his sermon like so many brass tacks driven into a wood coffin. The restaurateurs of Soho folded their hands and translated the term into '*femme, femme, femme*,' '*grue, grue, grue.*'

Jules, praying for Jim Drover, thought of Kay. He joined her life to his (the tea urn and the counter and the cigarettes), her life of eight to five tending a machine, in a mutual dissatisfaction. He wanted to release her, to release Drover. Always in the badly lit church, surrounded by the hideous statues of an uncompromising faith, listening to the certainty of that pronouncement – *péché, péché, péché* – he was given confidence, an immense pride, a purpose. However lost in the café, forgetful of knives and sugar, here he was at home.

When the Host was raised, Jules remembered, in the cave of his hands, the letter he had left unopened. Here in the middle of the only France he knew, the nuns and the prostitutes and the restaurateurs and the statues, he was filled with curiosity by this message from the real France. In the café the day before he had been uninterested, all his mind absorbed with the need of remembering things, but in the church while the wine was made blood, the most unlikely things seemed possible, emotion came easily, the desire for sacrifice, the desire for love, the desire for tenderness. It was as if a stranger whom he had long admired from a distance had asked him the time. The typewritten envelope was reassuring; his country was not importunate in its tenderness; no personal hand had passed him an appeal. In twenty minutes Mass would be over; I will go back and open the letter. But no, he told himself, I am going to see the priest about the petition.

Domine, non sum dignus. . . . Domine, non sum dignus. . . . Domine, non sum dignus. . .

He thought of his mother, how she had beaten him for what she called 'French ways', for his sudden raids into the

140

larder, his debauch among the sultanas. She had impressed on him that he was English now, that the English did not steal, that the English were serious, counted their money at night, and earned money only by hard work. Regularly every week she lost two shillings on a horse, and regularly she impressed on Jules that the English did not gamble. Regularly she told him that the English did not drink, regularly once a month he heard through the thin wall the hiccups in the neighbouring room. Regularly she told him that the English never thought of sex, regularly he heard the moans between the hiccups, for the man in France, the husband whom Jules supposed did all that the English thought should not be done, gambled and drank and laughed and looked at women and did not count the money for which he had not worked. He would have liked to know his father, but no word came from that paradisal land, even when his mother died.

Ite missa est.

When Mass was over, Jules went to the vestry to find the priest, but he was surrounded by Knights of Columba, stout elderly men with slips to their waistcoats, who were talking of rummage sales, whist drives, lantern lectures. I will catch him, Jules thought, after benediction. He walked quickly home and up to his room and opened the letter.

For some time he failed to understand it. He did not recognize his disreputable absconding father under the name of Heysan-Bretau, for his mother had altered their name at once to Briton. Nor was it like his father to be dead, after the proper rites, without pain, buried in the Catholic cemetery at Petit Tourville, 'mourned by his fellow townsmen and fellow councillors'. Jules was a little cast down; it seemed wanting in respect to have thought of him so lately gambling, drinking, making love. He had certainly counted his money; his solicitor spoke with cold formality of how respected his father had been, how no local tradesman had contributed

141

more generously during his life to charity, how in the coming year he would have been Mayor of Petit Tourville. The black-coated phrases conveyed no pictures to Jules of life in a small town, of Sunday Mass, of municipal politics. This respected figure, so nearly 'our respected Mayor', made a last attempt to wander round the Eiffel Tower, slipping Napoleon coppers into cigarette machines, crossing himself before holy statues in grottoes decorated with oyster shells, making eyes at women, pinching their bottoms as he passed; not without a struggle did he slip into his six-foot hole while the Fire Brigade presented arms and the town council laid a wreath. Could his spirit have refrained from laughter at the thought of the hiccups and the moans of his deserted wife?

'A bequest of 10,500 francs to my son, Jules, trusting that he will invest the sum in sound Government securities and waste none of it in games of chance, gambling or the pleasures of the senses. The residue of my estate to be divided equally between the Governor of the Home for Indigent Trades-people, Petit Tourville, and the Pastor of the Church of Notre Dame, Petit Tourville, the interest in the latter case to be used to augment the annual income of the Altar Society.'

Ten thousand five hundred francs: it was about a hundred and fifty pounds. 'My God,' Jules said aloud: he began to laugh. He ran downstairs; there was no one in the café; I must celebrate; he called down to the kitchen: 'My father's dead,' and ran into the street. *Mon père est mort, vive mon père.* He ran back into the café and called up the stairs to Conder, but Conder was out. Kay, he thought, there's Kay; she'll love me today, nobody could help loving me today. I'm rich. I've got ten thousand francs. I'm happy. How to find her? We'll celebrate, we'll marry. I'll take a car, we'll ride into the country, we'll have lunch, tea, dinner together, we'll love each other, I'm so happy. She mustn't go to work tomorrow. I'm so happy. How can I find her? *Mon père est mort, vive mon père.*

He carried the paper round with him, he showed it to everyone; he felt that he had everything in the world he wanted. Everyone was kind to him and laughed with him. Yes, they said at the garage, he could have a car for the whole day, for the whole night if he wanted; it was just the day for a ride in the country, they said; the beechwoods out by Beaconsfield would have their autumn colourings; in Ashdown Forest the heather would be out. Yes, they said at the rooms in Dean Street, he could have them tomorrow if he chose; it was just the time of year to be married in, they said: 'a summer's child was healthy and wise'. Yes, they said at the Presbytery, if he got a special licence there would be no difficulty. Yes, they said at the café, they'd serve a wedding breakfast in the private room. It seemed to Jules that he had been very much alone, but that now he would never be alone again.

And then to crown the perfect day, his only difficulty was solved, and there was Kay smiling with bright lips outside Leicester Square Station. He could hardly believe his eyes; it was as if he had been rolling his life laboriously up, up a steep hill, and now it topped the rise and now it rolled before him faster and faster, so that he had to run to keep behind it, this gay, this fortunate life. *Mon père est mort, vive mon père.* She had been waiting for someone, she said, but he had not come. She had been waiting half an hour. She was tired of waiting. 'A hundred and fifty pounds. We are going to take a car. We are going into the country.' Everything was arranged; he had known somehow that he would find her.

'But I ought to wait – another five minutes.'

'Listen. Where shall we go, south, east, west, north?' He moved restlessly on the edge of the pavement; people stared at him; they pushed him on one side as they scrambled for their buses. He was longing to be out of London, somewhere quiet, away from the traffic, where he could tell her everything he had planned.

'You're crazy, Jules.'

'We'll go north. We shall get out of London so quickly then. Camden Town, Golders Green, Hendon, and there you are. No distance then to Berkhamsted, to Ashridge Park, Ivinghoe.' He had gone there two years ago in a side-car for a motor-cycle trial; it had been winter: red berries in the hedges and a thin rime sparkling on the downs; in the Park the grass had crackled under foot.

'But, Jules, I must be back quite early. Work at eight tomorrow.' He nearly told her then: you'll never go to work again, you're marrying me. I've got the room, I've ordered the breakfast, I've all but bought the licence. Something restrained him: a little inherent caution native to France, to Petit Tourville – 'Government securities – waste none of it in games of chance . . . the pleasures of the senses'. He thought that he was waiting till night; there were things expressed better in the dark, so that, 'You're crazy, Jules,' might sound like a caress, when 'I've such a lech for you' was passion and poetry.

It was not a large share of caution he had inherited; his driving was reckless. He could not keep his eyes on the road with Kay beside him. I shall never be alone again, he thought over and over again. In Camden Town he saw Conder walking rapidly down the pavement towards the Carreras Factory with his head bent and his hat in his hand; Jules shouted and waved his hand, but Conder did not see him, people were stepping out of his way, he seemed to see no one. They stopped for a drink at 'Jack Straw's Castle'. The dogs were yapping round the toy boats on Whitestone Pond, and an old man kept on saying that he could see St Paul's and nobody listened to him.

'But where are we going, Jules?'

144

'You'll see.'

Down into Golders Green and out to Hendon, the miles drummed out at seventy to the hour on the great curved road, down to the road house by Huntonbridge. They had lunch there, and again he nearly told her everything. But the waiter brought the cheese and the waiter brought the coffee and somehow there was no time to tell her that they were going to be married and live in Dean Street and have a wedding breakfast in the café's private room.

After lunch she was sleepy and curled up beside him, and he drove with one arm round her. It occurred to him, driving very slowly now, watching the hedges and the cows (near Boxmoor a barge drawn to the bank and the old horse feeding), that he had never before had quite this sense of happiness. He thought of his father with tenderness, who had given him Kay sleeping at his side and this autumnal drive with the old year dying and the old horse nodding and the old leaves rotting on the ground. In a field a blue smoke rose from a pyre of weeds which had been lit the evening before and burned gently still in the dry clear air. Cars continually outpaced them; but the joy of speed had left him; he ambled down the road and let high-powered screaming purpose vanish round the corner; he had no purpose beyond the preservation of this peace, beyond carrying peace gently like a precious vase into the evening. He had not been out of London since his drive to Ivinghoe two years ago, tossed in a side-car, silence shattered by the explosions of the exhaust.

In Berkhamsted purpose plunged down the High Street, roared past for Tring and dinner, Jules turned by the church, over the canal and under the railway bridge, along the moat and the fractured walls of the castle. As they climbed above the town, evening swept the common, the gorse, the clay, wounded by old trenches, the abandoned butts, and cast the hillside ferns in shadow. Kay slept and

145

moved and slept again and came awake. She said: 'It's cold.'

Jules was silent, driving with one hand. A woman moaned and drank and moaned; the earth was dry and a coffin was lowered and the Fire Brigade presented arms. Out of these two came happiness, came this particular evening sun flaming across the radiator, came this sense that never again would he be alone.

She was deliciously out of place in the Park, a little bored, a little puzzled, making up under a tree. It was almost too dark to see herself. She peered into her mirror and banged the compact shut. 'Listen, Jules, you must be sensible.'

He began to laugh at her; the grass had gone grey and a bird persistently called. 'Why talk about being sensible? You don't want to be sensible.'

'That's true,' she said thoughtfully. She looked at him with more interest than she often showed to a man. The men she usually companioned had money and did not work, or the work they did was something she could not understand because it was so highly paid, but Jules was like her in this, he had a boss, he went to work early and his hours were long. Mr Surrogate had said: 'Don't let's be sensible,' but he had not meant the same as Jules. He had meant, 'Sleep with me now and don't worry me later,' he drew her out of her own security while he remained himself quite safe in his warm lit flat. He hadn't, above all she resented that even while she lay with him, he hadn't to go to work in the morning. But Jules had. He was no more independent than she.

'All right,' she said, 'we won't be sensible.'

He clapped his hands and said: 'We won't go back to-night,' as if the idea had suddenly struck him. He did not let her know that, while she was washing in the cottage where they had tea, he had taken a room for the night. He was delighted that she did not take offence; only protested that she must be at work 'so early'. 'I'll drive you there,' he said.

146

Again he might have told her: you're marrying me, you're not going back to work, but the black-coated wisdom of the elderly tradesman restrained him.

'Will you love me?' They pressed against each other and protested and laughed and told indecent stories and were happy. The leaves crackled on the ground and a rabbit's tail flashed like a match under a bank of ferns and disappeared. When they held their breath it seemed to them both for a moment that they had never heard so deep a silence; they thought of London at night and how the heavy lorries shook the walls; 'So quiet,' she said, but already she was thinking: This is serious. I wanted him to do this to me after the meeting. I've never wanted a boy like this before. My God, I'm crazy. I've got to be careful or there'll be an accident.

'Not really quiet,' he said, taking his arm away from her, hearing the dogs bark in the village, the rustle among the leaves, the gentle fall of earth as an animal passed, the turmoil of insects. But one called this quiet, as one called darkness black; it was the nearest approach to silence. Even if the insects and the dogs were still, there was always the beating of one's own heart. He quite forgot her while he thought: even when I've been most alone, I've always had other things to listen to than my heart; I've never noticed it beating.

She slid lower against the tree trunk and said: 'How hot it is.' It was less than two hours since she had said: 'How cold,' but kneeling now she was in the shelter of the branches, and the dry crinkled leaves held warmth close to the ground like earth-browned hands sheltering a flame. She sucked the back of her hand which a stem had scratched and her lipstick left traces on the skin; she watched Jules with a hunger she had never allowed herself to feel before. He was lost again, peering over the bracken between the beeches, and she did not speak a word to help him find himself. She was willing that he should be lost a long time with his eyes a little dilated

147

and his breathing uneven and the hand which touched hers
as insensient as a stranger's in a crowded Tube. She could
feel herself for a few minutes abandoned with him, Milly's
demands on her forgotten.

But Jules' thoughts when they returned to her were practical. He suddenly laughed and put his hands on her shoulders and forced her lower in the bracken. The stems
scratched through her stockings, and as she resisted him, she
could feel the earth in her nails. 'Don't be a fool, Jules.' He
was on his knees too, forcing her back and laughing at the
same time. He was not strong, but he was quick and resili-
ent. He bit the lobe of her ear and pushed at her with his
head between her breasts. She remembered the lipstick in
her hand and smeared it across his face from nose to chin;
she began to laugh too; she could smell the bracken and the
earth mould and the Coty Naturelle and a spray of gorse in
bitter flower behind her. 'Stop,' she said, 'wait a bit. Let's go
indoors.'

He loosed her and sat back on his heels. 'That's a promise.'

'Why can't you wait till night?'

He grinned and made a little vulgar gesture with his
thumb. 'Ready for more tonight.' He began to whistle; he
tried to do a handspring, but put his hand on a thistle and
swore. He was happy, he was conceited, he was cocksure. He
had his girl. He said: 'Did you see Conder? Thank God, I'll
never be like him. I wouldn't be alone like that for anything.
I want company – always. I'd be afraid, alone like that.
I'd get fancies.' He flashed at her with comic hopefulness.
'You aren't a Catholic by any chance?' Easier, then, the
formality of marriage, more final the barrier against loneliness, an impregnable dyke till death; otherwise the sea
corroded.

'No,' she said, 'why?' She stretched her legs regretfully,
thinking: why didn't I play with him? It would be fresh like

this in the open. What are a few spiders when you're hungry? 'Why? Do you want me to marry you?'

He shied quickly away, got to his feet. 'I was just wondering, that's all.' Games of chance, the pleasures of the senses. . . . But it was absurd. He wanted her, not only at this moment but for ever, and why should a black-coated ghost, a solicitor, the distant voices of Petit Tourville restrain him? Government securities. Four pounds a year in interest. 'Listen,' he said.

'I'm not sure I wouldn't marry you,' Kay said. 'I'm fed up with gentlemen. They keep you waiting half an hour and then they don't turn up. He was fond enough of me last night, I can tell you.' Her disappointed senses found a little relief in the thought of the pink counterpane, the beautiful dead woman envying her pleasure from the wall. Jules listened with admiration. She was a catch, surely even that disappointing libertine, his father, must admit that she was a catch. She was young and pretty and practised; he could not imagine a wife who could more ably stir his senses. He felt no bitterness that he was not the first man she had known; one did not expect as much when wages were so low, employment so precarious, everything which made life worth living, the cinema, the dance hall, powder and scent and rouge and stockings, so dear.

He egged her on; he liked hearing her speak of marriage without realizing how close it was to them, how attainable. 'You wouldn't want to marry,' he laughed, and kicked an ant-heap and felt a curious freedom in the grey air. A leaf span down the wind and touched his cheek. He was in at the death of something old and he was happy.

'I might try it,' Kay said.

'You've got too many friends.'

'I wouldn't lose them. My husband would have to toe the line and shake hands. He'd get what he wanted at night.' It was the answer he had hoped for; he had no wish for any

149

intimate loneliness in love; he wanted uproar, new faces, parties at Southend. 'Meet Bill. This is Ern. Fancy you not knowing – ' Marriage was the switchback, the giant racer, the lobster teas, the guarantee that one would never be alone. He would even have welcomed her parents if she had had any; but they were both dead. He would never be one to say: 'Can't we be alone together?'; he had even bought Conder's company with the foreign coins he picked up on the café floor.

'You'd never be satisfied with one man.'

'Depends on the man.'

Loneliness was only too easily attained; it was in the air one breathed; open any door, it opened on to loneliness in the passage; close the door at night, one shut loneliness in. The toothbrush, the chair, the ewer and the bed were dents in loneliness. One had only to stop, to stare, to listen, and one was lost. Then sorrow gripped him for all the useless suffering he could do nothing to ease, he was torn by humility, he was desperate for a place in the world, a task, a duty. But give him voices, company, and he was happy, he was cocksure, he was vulgar, he showed off.

'You see what I can do.'

I've got to be careful, she told herself over and over again. This is when a girl gets a baby; when she's got a lech like this; when she doesn't take precautions; when she doesn't want to take precautions; when she's in love.

They were at the park gates. There was no moon. The dark was round them, but the lights of the car made a small friendly glow in the road. You could almost believe it was a fire to warm your hands at. 'Come on,' Jules said, and took her hand and ran towards the car. 'I'm in a hurry,' he said, thrusting her into her seat, climbing into his own without opening the door, pushing at the starter. Warmth passed between them as he pressed down his foot and she tried to quiet her own excitement by telling herself that this was only the echo of last night; of three months' abstinence. But there was this difference. Desire before had always been a form of coquetry; one was careful even if one wasn't good; she had never before been bitter because she must be careful, had never longed to be taken as she was, anywhere, anyhow, in the car, in the bracken, and damn the consequences. If we were married, she thought, if we had money, if we were married.

He had ambled all the way from Boxmoor, but now he drove wildly the dark road back to Ivinghoe. The trees shot up against the light and disappeared; a single cottage at a right-angled turn; a woman flat as cardboard at a gate. When the car came out on to the ridge of down, the wind snapped at them, got into their clothes, worried them like a dog. They left it behind, driving down behind the hump of the beacon. He said: 'This bus can move,' put his arm round her, accelerated. Kay laughed and pressed herself close to him and told him to go faster, faster, faster. The little needle waggled and climbed. 'I'm in a hurry.' You could see nothing but the splash of chalky road in front; you were alone in a small vibrating cage, with a blue light burning above the dial; you had never been in this car before today. Like a horse that feels the weakness of its rider's thighs, it had the mastery; it bucketed towards the centre of the road. 'Go on. Go faster.' They were both a little frightened; he knew the car was not completely under his control; she knew that he was scared. So she said: 'Go faster, faster,' daring herself and him. The cross-road at the bottom of the hill rushed up to them; she saw a light shooting along the hedgetops on their left and: 'Look out, a car,' and heard him fumbling at the brake. Two wheels lifted, she closed her eyes, and as the car shot diagonally across the road, prayed: 'My face, don't let it be my face.'

'Good driving that,' Jules said, and she opened her eyes while he continued to boast in an uncertain voice that there were not many drivers who would have avoided a collision. 'It gave those other fellows a start. If I'd lost my nerve – ' The arrow waggled, fell, the hedges bobbed slowly up and down, a farm, the first house. 'I believe you were scared,' Jules said. He took a cigarette out of his packet to show how unconcerned he was, but the match he struck wavered and went out. He forgot to light another because they had arrived.

He went on boasting all the way upstairs. He stood between the bed and the washstand and boasted. He was such a driver, he was such a regular fellow, he had nerve enough for two. She sat on the bed and made up her face and felt a faint nausea. He stretched out his hand to prove his words and she smiled when all the tension of his muscles could not prevent it shaking. 'You couldn't hold a tea-cup,' she said.

'You ought to be grateful,' he told her in his light cocksure conceited manner. 'That was driving.' She thought at first that like other men he was talking to hide his shyness, that he had lost his confidence now that he was alone with her, but he was boasting because he was happy, because he had been scared, because he had thought the car would crash and he would be alone again with Conder and the café. Never for a moment had it occurred to him that his own life was in danger. It was too vibrant now to be cut short like that, too certain of what it wanted.

'Jules,' she said. 'Jules, can't you wait?' but she had no wish to wait, she welcomed him: she only regretted the promptitude of the embrace when it was so quickly finished that it might have been no more than the gesture he had made her in the park, a salutation across the street. He was with her, he was in her, he was away from her, brushing his hair before the glass, whistling a tune.

'Oh, stop it,' she said. He glared at her; he had an idea that he had not satisfied, and he was irritated. He would

152

have been humiliated but for the thought that there were months and years ahead; they were going to marry; he would do better next time. The window was open, and he could smell bacon frying in the kitchen below. 'Eggs and bacon,' he said, 'I'm hungry.' He forgot for a moment what they had just been doing; there was so little to remind him of it, now that his body was quiet again.

She said: 'I'm not hungry,' sullenly.

'If only,' he said, remembering everything, the legacy, the drive, Kay on the bed, 'there was something to do. I don't know why we came out here. We might have gone to the pictures, had a party.' He spun round to the mirror to form a quick image of himself in a hired dinner jacket, opening a bottle, proposing a toast, shaking hands, 'meet my fiancée'.

'You could have had your friends in,' he said, 'and we'd have announced – ' but the concerted opinion of Petit Tourville restrained him. 'My legacy.'

Kay lay on her back with her legs crossed and her eyes half closed. She loved him and had found that he had given her less pleasure than many chance companions. You expected such a damned lot from love, a unique excitement, a quality of everlastingness; no value remained unshaken when love was this: Jules with you and then Jules further away than he had ever been, cute and cocksure and self-satisfied, studying his face in a mirror.

'You talk such a hell of a lot,' she said, 'about that legacy. £150 isn't much. I'd show you how to get through it inside a week. Why, I've known men who've earned that every week,' she said, lying desperately with the idea that if she could destroy his thought of the legacy, he would be once again Jules dissatisfied, Jules who had a boss and must work in the morning like herself, the hopelessly lost Jules, who waited outside a cinema, while she drove off with Mr Surrogate, inarticulate, with no realization that she was crazy

153

for him, that she was hungry, that she would love him anywhere, anyhow. 'Every week,' she said, 'God's truth I have.'

He blinked at her. 'Spend it in a week?'

'Any girl would show you.' She could not have pricked the bubble of his conceit more effectually. He left the mirror altogether and came to the foot of the bed; this was the Jules of the café, the Jules between the tea urn and the till, the Jules she loved. Never mind now that he had not satisfied her, she lay back and sighed with happiness, dreaming of the night and other nights. It was almost possible to believe that she might give up her friends for him; if he asked her, marry him. For a year or two they would be perfectly happy; she would not go to the factory; and then when they were no longer crazy about each other, thank God you could give each other up; a friend of hers had got a divorce for five pounds. But Jules was a Catholic. 'Do Catholics divorce each other?' She had not meant to speak aloud.

'No,' he said furiously, 'no.' It seemed to him that he had grossly exaggerated his love for her; it was a feeling one got until one had had the girl, and then it went; what was worse, he had exaggerated the value of his legacy. She was right; a girl could run through it in a week: his father was right: 'Government securities' – five pounds a year; it was better than spending it. He began to count up what he had already spent that day. If I drove her back now and cancelled the room. But he shrank from the loneliness of the night which would follow. Besides, he told himself, I have not decided. I can still ask her tonight, tomorrow morning.

'I'm going downstairs,' he said, 'to see if supper's ready.' He opened the door, loneliness was in the dark passage, he stumbled on the unlit stairs, loneliness round his feet. Even the room below with the table spread for their supper was empty, so that he turned to call to her: 'Come quick,' but thought better of it. The fire was laid, but needed a match.

He had no match and he felt in his pocket for a spill to light from the gas. This was not as he had intended: 'Meet Ern. Haven't you met, Bill? Don't you know – ' He could hear her moving slow-footed overhead, but he was satisfied in the body, he was uninterested. It was a very lonely state, satisfaction. He told himself again, I can always ask her tonight, but he knew quite well that he would be as silent on that subject as the room was silent, the passage, the stairs.

The petition paper for Drover's release crinkled into flame. He bent and held it to the fire.

*

It had needed all Conrad's courage to follow the resolution he had formed in the night, when he had lain awake and listened to Milly crying, even as far as the street. A policeman passed; it was odd how quickly one became afraid of the law, but when he had got what he wanted, he would fear no one.

What shall I do with it?
What excuse shall I give?
What's the good of it?'

But he had not had enough sleep to answer questions. Somebody touched his arm, pushed him a little to one side, and went on down the pavement. Again he felt the wild anger, the hatred, as when he heard the jokers outside the Berkeley. They didn't know me, they didn't notice me, but I know one of them all right, I'd seen him in court day after day, yellow in the face, old, worn-out, watching Jim in the dock, Jim who was young and fresh and as good as dead.

He put out his hand and pulled the bell and heard the iron jangle behind the barred and shuttered windows, behind the strips of scarlet print: 'Sale. Premises Damaged by Fire.' I've done it now, he thought, I've set something going that must go on, and a moment later while the echoes died, he was thinking again of the Assistant Commissioner and of how a word from that man might have saved Jim; if the police evidence had been given a little more sympathetically, if they had admitted to having clubbed women, the jury would have recommended him to mercy.

Then again Milly was in his arms, they were struggling in the bed, she was crying and close to him, he experienced the pitiful pleasure of their union.

'Mr Bernay?'

'Come inside.'

He was so absorbed in Milly's misery, the idea of how empty her life must be for her to accept his love, that he did not notice for some minutes Mr Bernay's secrecy and promptitude. It only came to him when he sat down opposite the long polished empty face and Mr Bernay asked him non-committally in what he could serve him: 'I don't think I know – ' He wore a black tail-coat and showed lengths of stiff white cuffs. These he presently shot with an air of getting down to business and remarked: 'I was just off to church.'

Conrad said: 'I see you have a sale of your old stock.'

'Damaged by fire,' Mr Bernay corrected him.

'Weren't you insured?'

'That's typical of me,' Mr Bernay said. 'I'm too sociable. I forget things. Your face now – '

Conrad said: 'You don't know me. I belong to the Regal Assurance Company,' and noted with pleasure a faint unease touch the wide white face, like the shadow of a man in a cinema crossing the empty screen.

Mr Bernay said: 'I don't know why you come to see me on a Sunday.'

'Privately,' Conrad said. 'I thought that as you'd had dealings with my firm, you might oblige me. I wanted to buy something cheap.'

Mr Bernay watched him and Conrad waited. He knew the kind of thoughts which were passing now through the other's head, and the knowledge gave him the sense of power. The other was neatly dressed, was well-off, was a Church-goer, wore starched cuffs on a Sunday, but a few words had rendered him speechless. Mr Bernay began to pick his nails.

'We were surprised,' Conrad said, 'that you didn't press your claim.'

'I couldn't wait,' Mr Bernay said, 'the damage was trifling: you insurance companies are so slow. What is it you want?'

'A revolver.'

Mr Bernay said: 'Of course, I have to see your licence. In any case, I don't believe I have one.'

'I haven't got a licence.'

'Why do you want one?'

'I'm so much alone.'

'Ah,' Mr Bernay said, leaning back behind the desk, grasping, as it were, with both hands this opportunity for assertion, 'I don't understand that. I, you see, am never alone.' His face was temporarily lighted by the lamps of innumerable social occasions. He permitted Conrad to glimpse vistas of red carpet, to stare like an outcast through the lit windows from his own darkness and loneliness. For he was lonely, as lonely as he had ever been in spite of his passion and what he would once have considered his success. There had been times when he had thought that to be a woman's lover would armour anyone against shame, when there had seemed promise of infinite confidence in one short movement. Now he knew that he needed more than a physical act. He wanted years together.

'Sometimes,' Mr Bernay said, 'I'd just like to creep away. Far from the madding crowd,' Mr Bernay said, shooting his cuffs. His large soft trustless eyes swept Conrad like a couple of arc lamps, picking out his misery and loneliness. 'There's such a thing,' Mr Bernay said, 'as too many friends.' He

157

pretended to envy Conrad his solitary condition as a parsimonious millionaire turns off a tramp with words of envy for his irresponsibility.

'The revolver,' Conrad said. But Mr Bernay had quite recovered; he was again the social figure. It was impossible to suspect that behind that blank respectable façade there had ever been a pawnbroker afraid of questions.

'You must get a licence. How can I tell what you might be up to? Violence. Anything. Look at the way you've come to me, on a Sunday when the shutters are up. And your hand. Look how it's shaking. Your nerves are all upset, you ought to have a tonic. You aren't fit to be out, let alone with a revolver.'

In the shop several clocks began to strike the hour. 'There,' Mr Bernay said. 'I'm too late for church.'

'Why should you have scruples?' Conrad said. 'I know all about you. I've handled all the papers about your fire.' It had seemed to him during the night a very easy thing to get what he wanted from the pawnbroker. It was to have been a kind of safe blackmail; he had pictured a very frightened dealer, not Mr Bernay with his cuffs and his patronage and his broad shining face and his blandness.

Mr Bernay said gently: 'I'll report you to your firm. You have driven me to it. I don't like doing harm to anyone. I'm as good a Christian as the next man.'

'I'm not asking you to do it for nothing.'

'It's your tone I dislike,' the pawnbroker said. 'I'd stretch a point for a friend (and I tell you there aren't many men with a bigger acquaintance than mine), when I wouldn't raise a little finger for an enemy. Not a little finger.' The large soft eyes seemed to push Conrad very far into the distance, until he was a minute figure on the very horizon of Mr Bernay's consciousness; with such a small figure one could do anything; raise a hand, it would be sufficient reproof, a smile would be sufficient forgiveness, or if one were, after all, to do business, somebody so inconsiderable could not complain at the hardest bargain.

'I didn't mean any harm,' Conrad said. It seemed to him now that he wanted the weapon more than anything else in life; he had wanted love, but he had had that; it was over.

'What do you want it for?'

'Against an emergency.' It was true; he had no clear idea of its use; there were people he hated, his fellow-clerks, the director's nephew, the manager, the police commissioner, the man who pushed him on the pavement, but he did not really want to kill these people any more than he wanted to kill himself. Less, because he had more reason to hate himself; he loved his brother and he had done his brother what people seemed to consider the bitterest of wrongs. It had been difficult to believe in the wrong during the commission; it had been so easy, so short, so lovely, so unsatisfying, but afterwards, awake and silent in bed, he had pasted the proper labels on his memory of it. 'A mortal sin.' 'The bitterest wrong.' 'A broken commandment.' But the labels were not his; he had taken them from others; others had made the rules by which he suffered; it was unfair that they should leave him so alone and yet make the rules which governed him. It was as if a man marooned must still order his life according to the regulations of his ship.

He entreated the pawnbroker, stretching a hand across his desk. 'As a favour. I might be able to help you at the office.'

'That's better,' Mr Bernay said, 'That's a better tone. People have got to learn that they can't threaten me. I'm as good a Christian as the next man, but I won't be threatened.'

'Please – ' Conrad said.

'What's wrong with you is nerves. You ought to take Sanatogen, see people, go about. I'm sixty-five,' Mr Bernay said, 'though I know you won't believe it. And I attribute my health more than anything to social life. I don't have time to think. Here to lunch and there to dinner. A ring on the 'phone.'

'Please – ' Conrad said.

Mr Bernay opened a cupboard without rising from his desk, swivelling his chair. He put a cardboard box in front of him and began to remove cameo brooches and cuff-links, a pair of spurs, an egg-cup and a dusty revolver. 'You'll have to pay me for the risk,' Mr Bernay said and smiled and checked the smile and blew his nose. 'Five pounds with a box of ten rounds.'

'A cheque.'

'Four pounds ten cash.'

'Will it work?' Conrad asked, and Mr Bernay began to recede very rapidly with his brows raised in interrogation. 'Work,' a voice said a long way off, 'of course it will work'; he was very hot and then very cold and then Mr Bernay ran smoothly back towards him, as if propelled from behind like a Guy Fawkes in a pram. 'Thank you,' he said and paid and struggled back as quickly as he could to the open air and heard the chains go back on the door and the bells ringing for Matins.

And now what? Conrad thought. What is this for? A joke to tell Milly, something with which to frighten people who push me on the pavement, who want my job, who call, 'Conrad, Conrad,' across the asphalt yard, who threaten me, who hang my brother, who do not (that was the worst crime) take me seriously, as a man, as a chief clerk, as a lover. You cannot frighten me with the name of murderer; a murderer is only Jim; a murderer is strength, protection, love.

When a cannibal ate his enemy, he received his enemy's qualities: courage or cunning. When you lay with your brother's wife, did you not become, receiving the same due as he received, something of the same man, so that if you were weak, you became strong, clever, you became stupid?

160

For an instant last night he had been his brother, he became capable of killing a man.

The impetus of that belief returned to him, carried him down Shaftesbury Avenue, across Trafalgar Square, halfway down Northumberland Avenue before it left him without the faintest idea of what he had meant to do. A policeman saluted, a door slammed, and up a by-street towards him the Assistant Commissioner came walking, umbrella over his arm, a file of papers in his hand.

He came, yellow-lined face; he came, thin bureaucratic body; he came slowly, justice with a file of papers; he came, respectability with bowler hat and umbrella; he came, assurance, eyes on the pavement, safe in London, safe in the capital city of the Empire, safe at the heart of civilization ('I see no reason to reverse the judge's decision'; the raised truncheon; the forbidden meeting; 'after one year we allow them to embrace'; reduced staffs, unemployment; the constant struggle with your fellow man to keep alone upon the raft, to let the other drown; desire; adultery; passion without tenderness or permanence); down the street the upholder of civilization, eyes on the pavement, neat file under his arm.

A word from him, Conrad thought, and Jim would live; a word from him to the Home Secretary, that his police were out of hand at the meeting. And it seemed to him that he might appeal personally, here in the street, to the Assistant Commissioner. He was walking slowly; but in half a minute he would be close enough to touch. Conrad trembled at the approach of authority; always in managers' rooms he had to hide behind him the trembling of his hands, while he waited for a reprimand, for dismissal; the trembling did not cease at unexpected words of praise or of promotion.

I daren't speak to him.

He put his hands into his pockets to hide them and felt the rough rusty chamber of the revolver. With this in my hand

161

I ought never to be afraid again; I have only to point this and others will fear me; even that old flat face would be afraid. The Assistant Commissioner was beside him; was passing him, crepitating a little in his old-fashioned boots and stiff Sunday clothes like a yellow grasshopper.

Conrad put out a hand. 'Sir. . . . One moment.'

*

The Assistant Commissioner hesitated, went on, his whole bearing altered; he was an officer inspecting barracks, stiff with resentment at some breach of convention, which some-one would later hear about; one could not reprimand a junior officer before the ranks – the ranks were the cabmen in their taxis, the waiting charabanc load.

It's disgraceful, the Assistant Commissioner thought, a respectably dressed man like that begging. He can be thankful I didn't put him into custody, but he had hardly turned into Northumberland Avenue before his attitude changed. His business was not justice; his business was only to catch the right man; but in private, in his secret life, he was troubled by the slightest deviation from the strictest justice. In private life one could not leave justice to the Home Secretary, to Parliament, to His Majesty's Judges; possibly to God, but the Assistant Commissioner was not fully satisfied of His existence. Now again he had forgotten that unemployment was not a mark of the lazy man; that the beggar did not beg because he would not work; that had once been the case in the England he knew best, but things were different now.

The Assistant Commissioner turned and went back. He was anxious to apologize for his attitude, to give the poor man half a crown, but when he got to the corner the man had gone. The Assistant Commissioner was perturbed; there had been no need of harshness. What was it that made one recoil from a beggar, shut up the face and hurry on? It was

162

partly sympathy; one did not care to look at a man in such straits; but the beggar could hardly be expected to understand that turning away was a form of sympathy. The Assistant Commissioner stood at the corner as if he had forgotten something. In fact he had remembered; he had had a vision of the innumerable shut faces which a beggar sees. I wish I had spoken to that man, the Assistant Commissioner thought, I wish I had asked him how he came to be unemployed; it might have been possible to find him work; but what good after all would that have been? he is only one; it is impossible for me to help these men, only the State can do that, the State which employs me to keep order, to see that the unemployed beg and do not demand.

The Assistant Commissioner told himself that this train of thought was doing him no good; I'm paid; I've got to do my job. One did not question during the war why one fought; one waited till the war was over for that. I can think about these things when I retire; but the idea of retirement chilled him. He turned his back on the source of his perplexity and walked up towards Trafalgar Square. He wished he had had these new reports sent by messenger to his flat, not fetched them himself as an excuse for a walk on a fine Sunday morning. The men on duty at the Yard would never believe that to be his only reason, a liver that had to be nursed, legs that needed exercise, a glittering autumn morning with the bells ringing.

He turned his back on the spot where the man had stood, but his thoughts were too slow for him easily and quickly to escape from any one of them. When I retire. Once after three days in the jungle, steaming heat and one of his men stabbed and the ration of water nearly exhausted and the men they pursued as far away as ever, they had broken with relief out of the trees into the clearing where a trading station stood; here they could get fresh water, rest, eat, talk. It was the end of their jungle pursuit; from the station a rutted road, at

163

least as good as an English country lane, drove straight for miles. Over the station (a bungalow, a tin-roofed store, a couple of native huts), a yellow flag dangled; there was no wind, the place seemed deserted, the flag hung like a sausage from its pole and at first he did not notice its colour. It meant, of course, fever, a wide berth to water, rest, talk at that particular station. They had to march by at the edge of the clearing, down the straight rutted road, and it seemed hours before the flag ceased to be visible. Now it was the man with his hand out, begging, the thought 'when I retire', which hung like a yellow flag in his rear; useless to walk faster; there it stayed.

The Assistant Commissioner remembered that before the buildings dropped behind a haze of heat, he saw a man come out of the bungalow and move about the huts. He was strongly tempted to return; he could send the men on under his native sergeant; he could have rest, something to drink, and if he caught the fever, he would be able to dismiss for ever the fear of retirement. It was characteristic of him that the idea of saving a man's life weighed a little with him, the thought that his return might be considered meritorious never occurred to him at all. Finally he dismissed the idea as an indulgence; it was not what he was paid to do; he was not paid to risk his life in that way, but to punish and to preserve. Certainly he was not paid to escape retirement. Maddeningly every time he looked back there dangled the yellow flag.

He had been tempted once more before he left the East; one hot day in the capital, escaping from the glare and the glitter of the temples, the reflection of the sun on pieces of tin, old petrol cans and squares of coloured glass, he became aware in the dim overhung shaded street that he was followed. It was not exactly a sound that warned him, though unconsciously he may have picked out from the pad of oxen, the cries of vendors, a certain recurrent rhythm of soft feet persisting at a distance, persisting round corners, persisting when he crossed the road; but what he noticed was a physical uneasiness, an inclination to stoop. He knew of no particular reason why anybody should want to attack him; there were always general reasons, political reasons; he was the paid servant of an unpopular government. He was seriously tempted to walk on, turn down an even more shaded road; he did nothing of the kind, he went back to the main street and stopped the first car he saw.

The fountains rose, unfurled and dropped through sunlight. Elderly men in top hats hurried late into St Martin's-in-the-Fields; two barelegged children dipped their feet into the pool of a fountain and scrambled away as a policeman came across the Square. The Assistant Commissioner stopped him. 'A little – er – latitude today, constable,' he said, 'turn, turn your back when you can.'

Up to the National Gallery; along Pall Mall. He could not help a momentary pride in London, the gentle gleam of autumn on the buildings, the gentle movement of Sunday in the streets, only one bus in sight, nobody hurrying. All the buildings in sight had dignity and proportion; the boots was shaking a carpet outside Garland's Hotel. It was something to realize that the defence of this city was in his hands; it was easy to imagine for a moment that its enemies were all outside, that evil did not naturally belong in this peace, this ease and contentment, that the death at Streatham was a successful foray from the country; but always he had only to turn and the yellow flag would be there, dangling in his rear. The war which he fought was a civil war; his enemies were not only the brutal and the depraved, but the very men he pitied, the men he wanted to help; if he had done his duty the unemployed man would have been arrested for begging. The buildings seemed to him then to lose a little of their dignity; the peace of Sunday in Pall Mall was like the peace which follows a massacre, a war of elimination; poverty here had been successfully contested, driven back on the one

165

side towards Notting Hill, on the other towards Vauxhall.

But the Assistant Commissioner, like Pilate, washed his hands; justice is not my business; politics are not my business. God help the men responsible for the way that life is organized; I am only a paid servant, doing what I am told; I am no more responsible than a clerk is responsible for the methods of the business he serves. He had only his pay on which to live; it had been hard to save in the East; he had preserved nothing but the gourds, the native weapons, the sentimental débris of a hard career. It often occurred to him that he was less the general in control than the private soldier fighting in a fog, like the men at Inkerman, in a fury of self-preservation.

Up the Haymarket, along Jermyn Street, past the Turkish baths and the shuttered haberdashers', walking for the sake of exercise, for the sake of his liver; at least he could show that wound in evidence of zeal to his employers. With that sneer, unlike him in its bitterness, his thoughts reached the edge of the jungle through which for years they had toiled and hacked their way. The progress he made was slow, but it was not the first time he was aware of a thinning of vegetation. In the clearing would be water, rest, talk; would be the glimpse of an organization of life he need not serve for pay, which would win his fidelity by its fairness, its rationality, its just distribution of reward. But at the edge he inevitably turned back to the jungle; he was afraid of disappointment, the yellow flag; he was afraid too of the demands which might be made on him; he was old, he had a habit of life.

He was almost glad when he realized that he was being followed. To be followed was previously part of his profession and he was not at ease in his new life, at one remove from the battle he fought. He was not afraid, though the knowledge came to him in a physical form, a stooping of the back; the things he feared were all intellectual, questions,

166

doubts, suggestions. It pleased him too that the walk which had been taken merely for the benefit of his health should be given a professional interest. He turned sharply up St James's Street, walked rapidly towards the Circus, took the turning by Fortnum & Mason's and waited. A policeman passed, several women, and then a flood of people coming out from morning service at St James's. It was useless to try to identify his follower.

The Assistant Commissioner walked slowly to the Circus, went slowly downstairs into the subway, walked slowly, watching the reflections behind him in the shop windows, into the circular parade. It was almost empty; the woman policeman did not recognize him. The Assistant Commissioner suddenly increased his pace and made a complete circle very rapidly. He made a mental note of a man in dark clothes who stood in a telephone box with his back turned. Then he climbed thoughtfully up to the pavement by the London Pavilion and bought two papers.

It's odd, he thought, very odd; I must be mistaken. Why should he have followed me this distance? My memory's played me false; after all, I didn't see his face. I must see his face. But now that his consciousness was aroused, his instinct failed him. He could not tell whether he was any longer followed; impossible among all the footsteps on a London pavement to pick out a pair more persistent, more purposeful or more secretive than the rest. As he turned into the cocktail room of Lyons' Corner House he was convulsed with dry amusement, but he did not allow himself to smile. I'm being driven into queer places this morning, he thought, and studied the menu with disapproval and distaste. Concoctions! He said with secret irony, 'Can you let me have a – a whisky and – er – soda?' and pushed the bowl of potato crisps to the furthest limit of the table. Eating between meals!

He looked round him; the small room was nearly full; but

167

the man who had been in the telephone box was certainly not here. The Assistant Commissioner would have welcomed his presence; they had something in common; but here he was not at home. His surroundings gave an impression of shrillness and bright colour, and the air seemed full of the boasts of owner-drivers. He felt conspicuous because of his age and because he was alone. If his follower had come in he would have invited him to his table.

As he had to pass the time somehow, he opened the portfolio and took out the latest Drover reports. They were too contradictory to mean anything at all. He scowled at his glass of whisky and thought: this is not my job. Men seemed to be increasingly unwilling to accept their proper responsibilities. The Minister had the full report of the trial, the judge's notes; why must he try to shift the responsibility for hanging or reprieving a man on to someone else? He was afraid of the strike continuing a few days longer, of more taxes, of a Government defeat; the secretary had been quite frank, but it was a frankness which reminded him of a certain business man he had interviewed a few months ago at the Yard. He, too, had been frank; he had admitted frauds on the income tax amounting to more than twenty thousand pounds; he had (he said so himself) laid all his cards on the table. What it was he concealed the Assistant Commissioner never found out.

Nor would he ever know what motive, even shabbier, he supposed, than the ones named, the Minister had for hesitation. The Assistant Commissioner remembered grimly the medical certificates produced at the director's trial, how the Income Tax authorities had accepted twelve shillings in the pound to save the director from bankruptcy, to save him from a nervous breakdown. When he thought of the heavy sentences passed on men who stole a little jewellery from a rich man's house, the Assistant Commissioner was more than ever thankful that justice was not his business. He knew quite well the cause of the discrepancy; the laws were made by property owners in defence of property; that was why a Fascist could talk treason without prosecution; that was why a man who defrauded the State in defence of his private wealth did not even lose the money he had gained; that was why the burglar went to gaol for five years; that was why Drover could not so easily be reprieved – he was a Communist. Again, it was not his business; he resented having to report to the Minister that in his opinion neither the reprieve nor the execution of Drover would have any public effect. I shall send in no report till Tuesday, the Assistant Commissioner thought, they can wait for it. It's not my duty to put on the black cap.

He had never wanted to leave the East; his duty there had been plain; he caught murderers and thieves. There was no interference with justice by politicians or business men; it had been like an old-fashioned war; you fought in person; you did not sit at headquarters.

He sighed and drank his whisky and got up. Younger men, he thought, might live to serve something in which they believed. They would think of him with slight contempt, as of one who had not the courage of his convictions. His answer was that he had caught the murderer of an old woman in Paddington, that one day soon he would catch the Streatham murderer; that was what he should be judged by; not by the general standard of justice.

He stood for a moment at the door. He could see no one, and he began to believe that either his instinct had deceived him, or else that the shadowing was over. He could imagine no motive for it; here, thank God, he was not mixed up in politics. He left behind him with relief the coloured drinks, the belted coats, the tinted mouths, the potato chips, and walked home. Down Charing Cross Road he was not disturbed by the dead peace after a massacre; Edith Cavell with white lips and sightless eyes and prim rectitude stared across at the pavement artist; under the statue of Henry Irving a man was selling patent medicines. The fountains played and the children paddled and the constable turned his back. The Assistant Commissioner raised his hat to the Cenotaph without remembering even for a moment his battered company coming back through the mud at Passchendaele. He walked out into the road to avoid a ladder and touched a piece of wood when he thought: I was mistaken, certainly I was mistaken. One had to choose certain superstitions by which to live; they were the nails in the shoes with which one gripped the rock. This was what a war threw up: a habit, a superstition, one more trick by which one got through the day. The Assistant Commissioner bought poppies, took the outside of the pavement, was silent for two minutes a year, touched wood, drank soup from the side of the spoon, raised his hat to the Cenotaph. It was as well to be conventional when one fought so fierce and so indecisive a war; one's thoughts had to be canalized: Streatham, Paddington, wireless inventions, these principally held the mind, so one bought a poppy and saved the time which might have been wasted on the dead; one raised a hat and forgot the done-with past; one wore one's school tie and dispensed with introductions; one touched wood and saved the harassing and useless thought: perhaps I am wrong.

Along the Embankment and into Great College Street, and mechanically before putting his latch-key into the door, he turned his head. No one was in sight; he did not register the thought because no person, unexplained, was ever in sight; but when he was in the dim hall, among the steel engravings, he did not go up the stairs to the flat, but decided on a final test, opened the front door again and stepped out on to the pavement. There on the opposite side of the street stood the man in clerk's clothes who had put out his hand to beg. But it could not have been money he wanted, the Assistant Commissioner thought, and stood quietly in front of the door to allow the man to approach him. He looked white and tired and sick and could have alarmed no one; it was impossible to watch him without pity. The Assistant Commissioner took a step towards him and the man turned and went, disappeared round the corner without hurry; he seemed too tired to hurry, too hopeless to have an object in hurrying.

*

Conrad convicted himself of cowardice. It was only one more conviction. He had already convicted himself of lust, incompetence, ingratitude. The act which was to have been his armour against life, the secret inner pride, 'Even I am loved,' had betrayed him, and driven him along streets too many to count, had trailed him like a dusty coat behind the Assistant Commissioner. Milly, too, had betrayed him; she had given him the only thing he wanted, a thing he had never had the least hope of obtaining, and it had proved: something lovely over too quickly, weeping in the night, sleeplessness, condemnation, despair. He clenched his hands in a fury of useless hatred.

He could not discover whom he hated. His brother stared at him through the glass, whispered through the wire: 'Look after Milly.' Conrad leant closer and begged him not to despair: the appeal, the petition. His brother shook his head like an old dog with canker. 'It's Milly I'm worried about.' He seemed unable to think about his own death; anxiety was greater than fear; he seemed haunted by his responsibility for Milly. A missionary tapped the screen in the stove-heated schoolroom with a long pointer, begged with passion: 'Look at these,' and the children stared back with uncomprehending eyes, expressions of bored and stubborn stupidity; impossible to convey to them that these flat figures flashed one after the other upon the white sheet, naked, thin, bony-kneed, were children themselves; only

Conrad knew, only Conrad felt the unbearable responsibility for their starvation, could not forget them, though soon they were overlaid with foliage, with grinning chiefs smoking pipes, with a view of the Victoria Nyanza.

Milly came down the church while the electric drills rattled in the High Street, and she peered sideways on the look-out for an enemy.

Conrad dug his nails into his palms and tried to see himself in the window of a shop in Parliament Street. People are looking at me, he thought; there's something wrong with my appearance. He took out a handkerchief and rubbed his face: it may be dirt. He circled on the empty pavement before the shop front: my shirt may be hanging out; with shocked horror, my trousers may be open. He leant forward and stared so closely at his reflection that the glass touched his forehead. He would not look at himself directly; that would be indecent; it would be like examining a naked body; nor would he think of Milly directly, Milly lying back across the bed, hungry and unhappy and reaching for him; his mind reeled away from it to distant reflections of Milly, to a trodden slipper slapping the floor, to the smell of anthracite and the sound of drills, to the starved naked children on the screen.

But you are all right, his image seemed to say, your hat is straight, your tie is straight, your shirt tucked in. There is no dirt on your face. Your clothes are neat and suited to your station. There is no reason at all why people should turn and look over their shoulders at you. He circled in front of the mirror and a small boy laughed and a woman stared at him across the street.

They know I'm full of hate, he thought with an obscure and aching grief, as if he were a judge, aware of his own secret sin, who must still sit there and condemn; they are frightened of me, they are trying to drive me mad. It was a devilishly clever method, to stare and stare, and encourage others to stare and stare, till you thought your face was dirty, or your shirt hanging out, and found it was not that at all; and then the only explanation could be that you were behaving oddly and never knew it. Perhaps, he thought, all this time I am speaking aloud, and he tried to listen to himself, but was unsatisfied by the apparent silence and went back to the window to see whether his lips were moving. They were quite still, but that was not a final proof, for he remembered ventriloquists whose lips never stirred but the voice came. I may be shouting from windows all down the street, he thought; that is why I can hear nothing; I am out of hearing of my own voice.

He began to walk very rapidly up towards Trafalgar Square. He had never seen ventriloquists move about; they sat on dining-room chairs and held dolls, and sometimes people thought of numbers and the dolls guessed the numbers. He considered seriously, I should be good at that, being an accountant, and presently quite forgot his fear. It was as if his madness had been a little fume of smoke which had coiled upwards and now subsided and burnt unobtrusively at the bottom of his mind.

But the sense of guilt remained, and it seemed to him that it was of the guilt people were aware and not of the madness. It irked him; he wanted to get rid of it. It grew inside him as sexual unrest sometimes grew, until he had to go into the street and buy a woman and then after awhile he was at peace again, except for the dim conviction that this was not the way a man should live. It occurred to him that hate perhaps could only be dispelled in the same way, by giving way to it, and a strange homesickness overcame him for the moment when the Assistant Commissioner had come out of his door to watch him across the street. Then he had had only to press a trigger. It was almost as if he had missed happiness for ever in Great College Street, and he recalled the opportunity for murder with the same poignant sadness

173

as a city-bred child might remember a field of grass or corn.

People came out of churches after long sermons, putting on gloves, looking for taxis, impatient for lunch. Clocks struck and moved on and struck again; the crowded buses plunged down the street towards Kew and Richmond. Conrad felt no hunger; in any case he had no money with which to buy food, all but a few pence of his week's salary had gone into the pawnbroker's pocket. But he could not go back, because if he went back all would inevitably happen again: passion, sleeplessness, condemnation, despair. He would not even have the excuse that he loved her, for he loved her no longer; he had loved Milly riding on bus tops to Kew, in the next seat at the cinema, talking with frightened bravery, with harmless malice in the kitchen; but now he did not dare to think of her, but of the trodden shoe, the black children, the murmur of the gas. Even these images had power to repel him and to draw him to them; the trodden shoe spoke of the insecurity of his love, the whispering fire was home, was safety, was an absence of thought. They filled his mind, he saw nothing else: Piccadilly was a shoe, Knightsbridge a fire. The distance he walked all through the afternoon could only be judged by the tiring of his feet; he could not tire his hatred. He grew more clearly than ever aware that he could only rid himself of that in one way.

And yet there remained, even below the hatred, the belief that if he had been able to love naturally and without shame, if he had been loved with tenderness and permanance, there would have been no need of the pistol in the pocket, the aimless walking and the guilt. A green chair was close to him and he sat down; immediately someone came and asked him for money. He withdrew a hand from a trouser pocket with five pennies in the palm, and the man took two and went away; Conrad could hear his feet crunch on the gravel;

174

every time they paused a bell rang. There were other noises; he might have been at the edge of a great army hidden by mist; and for a moment it was not a shoe, a fire, a lantern slide which held his thoughts, but a faint memory of his secondary school, of a Latin lesson, of an army which waited on a hillside above a lake while an invisible enemy marched in the mist below. Suddenly the mist had cleared –

He saw a nurserymaid leading a child across a grassy plain, a Guardsman in uniform leaning over railings, a girl with puffed sleeves and long thin legs trailing a borzoi down a gravel path. Dogs were barking, children were shouting, and two lovers lay and whispered in the grass behind him. He sat alone, with hate curled inside him, and envied them all, the shouting children, the barking dogs, the lovers whispering. A man pushed a perambulator down the gravel and four children hung along the sides, impeded the wheels, stumbled and cried and talked. It seemed to Conrad that he was watching a great victory; this stranger was not alone, he would never be alone, not only in the sense that he was the centre of a crowd but because the crowd included him and recognized his existence: they asked him questions, they complained to him, they demanded his approval. Even the harassed face was, in Conrad's eyes, a token of victory: a conquering general is not free from care.

The lovers whispered, and the girl with the borzoi raised a gauntleted hand and waved to someone whom Conrad could not see, and the sunlight lay flat on the flat glass. The gravel was like gold and the light flooded under the lowest bar of the palings. In ten minutes it would be dusk and the nurserymaids would stand up with the perambulators under the trees, calling to the children to come in to supper (a glass of milk and two petit beurre biscuits) and bed with a night-light burning and the sun sunk out of sight below the Park and the horses going home and the lamps being lit and the

175   *social control*

cars drawn waiting to the kerb, like black cats crouched on a narrow leaden roof.

Conrad sat and nobody stared at him, nobody looked over a shoulder, nobody laughed; his clothes were properly adjusted, his face clean, his voice unheard. But he was embittered now because he was unregarded. It was as if he were dead and his unhappy ghost unable to communicate some incomprehensible wish belonging to the past. He got up; nobody looked at him; the girl with the borzoi had disappeared; the lovers were quiet because the shadows were reaching them, because soon it would be dark enough to be happy in; the nurserymaids were going back to Bayswater. He banged his fist on the paling and ran his nails along the bar, but nobody looked at him. The desire to grip a sleeve, to say, 'I am alive like you,' was almost irresistible; for if one were dead and so unhappy, there would be no hope left, no comfort – 'one day I shall be dead.' But these were fancies; at the same depth as his hate he knew that he was alive; for if this had been death, he would not have envied Jim; this was life which Jim was escaping, into which persistently, with a love indistinguishable in its effect from hatred, they were trying to push him back.

But no, he was wrong again. He was giddy, leaning across the paling, allowing the grass to shift and return, as the pawnbroker's face had receded and approached. This wasn't the life into which Jim might be thrust. That life did not include Milly.

He thought that nothing would induce him to return to Battersea; one was not driven to return to someone one did not love. One returned home, for that should mean comfort, tenderness, knowledge, understanding. These were things it was impossible, once experienced, to do without; but one could dispense with the satisfaction of a crude hunger, one could dispense with shame. But a dog, he thought, returns to its vomit. If I'm not careful, I'll be back where my brother's so often been before me.

That was the distance he had travelled from her in a night. Before their bodies had known each other, they had been closely acquainted; they had even shared something, their nerves and their suspicion, in which Jim had no part at all; she had sneered at him, as she sneered at all the world except his brother, but the sneers were without malice. He could believe that she loved him in a way, and that way, though it promised no satisfaction, was better than this shared lust, this shared ignorance of anything beyond a touch, a sense of physical closeness, a heat and a movement.

You began it, he accused her, rubbing his fist along the paling, but never again, never again. He was determined to sleep out, but in the darkness and the autumn cold, he was turned from the Park by a man who rang a bell. The motor-cars purred away, running softly; the Guardsmen walked away down Knightsbridge with their canes under their arms; the amateur whores were drinking coffee at the stall.

Conrad walked back up Piccadilly; every policeman stared at him, every woman grinned. The old game began again; they conspired to make him mad. It would be a bad look-out for them, he thought, if I were really mad, with a revolver in my pocket, and suddenly he knew why they all looked at him: the bulge and hang of his pocket told what he carried. They could see through the cloth; perhaps there was a hole and the metal shone. Presently, he thought, they will stop me and take it away, and I shall be able to do nothing with it after all. He had not yet decided what he would do with it, but if he could find a quiet place and sleep a little, he would be able clearly to consider its uses. It began to rain, a cold stinging rain close to hail; the people sheltering under the Ritz arcade stared at him: a policeman came down the pavement, watching him. It was as if they all envied him the power he carried. He did not dare to stay in one place lest they should rob him of it.

But the rain went on, he was drenched below the knees, and his back began to stiffen with rheumatism. He walked to keep warm and he only got more wet. It occurred to him that he might go to his old lodgings, but his landlady would be in bed, and he had not enough money to pay his fare all the way. The fire would be out, he would hang his dripping clothes over a chair and all night the drops would fall over the linoleum, and in the morning in damp clothes he would have to go to work. The director's nephew would talk and laugh among the clerks, and if cautiously he opened the door of his inner room, he would hear his voice: 'A night on the tiles.' Then the manager would pass through the clerks' room and hear what was said and be aware of the hidden current of mockery. He would ring his bell, as the man in the Park had rung his bell, and speak to him in front of his secretary, Miss Batlow, lean, elderly Miss Batlow with pince-nez, who fumbled in the files. The rain dripped from the canopy of the Criterion.

'Discipline, Drover, discipline. We must have someone who can keep discipline' – one hand on his telephone, another tapping a pencil,' and presently the director's nephew in his place in the inner room.

There was always suicide. That would solve the problem of how to stay out and keep dry, the problem of his rheumatism, the problem of how to keep his black-striped trousers neat. 'There is one thing we value very highly in an employee, Drover: neatness.'

He dived out suddenly, recklessly, into the rain. Neatness, I'll show them. The water splashed up above the kerb as the taxis came by from the theatre; it drummed on the umbrellas and scattered the lamplight like oil on the black surface of the street. It ran from the brim of his hat behind his collar; when his foot turned on the slippery pavement a pain ran inwards at his spine. It was difficult to know what kept him alive; he had no ambition, work was only a grim struggle to survive; the only man he loved was locked away from him; the only woman he had ever loved had shown him exactly what love between a man and a woman was worth. But it was that short pleasure which made him pause; it seemed nothing when it was first over, when he was ashamed and Milly cried and the walls shook and day came. Then the betrayal of his brother seemed everything. Hours passed and the body stirred again and pleasure, however short, seemed more important than a scruple. If I were stupid enough, he thought with envy, I should go back now; I'd forget everything but meeting her again; if she were stupid, she'd be wanting me now, forgetting everything, even Jim, in her hunger; if we were stupid, like Jim, we'd not care a damn about anything but the moment.

But she's no more stupid than I.

The rain drove between lamp and lamp and made the street dark. A bus drove down and stopped at the kerb beside him, like a small lit house in which people sat and talked and were warm before a fire; the lights on the wet pavement flickered like the gas flames in asbestos towers.

'Battersea,' somebody said (he thought it was the conductor). 'Last bus.' He sat in it and tried to see through the steaming windows Shaftesbury Avenue unwind behind them.

'Is this the last bus?' he asked, and the conductor said: No. There were many more. It was hardly eleven yet. But it was too late, Conrad thought, to do anything now. He was going back – like a dog to its vomit, he told himself again, for I'm not stupid enough to think that when this is over anything will be changed: it will all happen again, self-condemnation and despair. I'll be happy for ten minutes. If she has any sense, she'll have locked the door of her room; she can't lock the hall door, for it's broken.

A police boat went gently down the stream, burning a red light, and disturbed a sleeping gull which beat up through the rain to the level of the bus windows, then sank again on rigid wings into the dark and the silence, while the sheets of rain fell between.

If she has the sense – but he would not expect more sense from her than from himself, and he had come back. Pushing open the broken door and letting the rain drive after him into the hall, he saw her at once sitting on her bed with her frock off and her shoe slapping on the floor and her bony knees and her starved face.

She said: 'I was afraid you weren't coming back. Kay's not come home. She's away with some man. I couldn't bear to be alone.' The uncompleted form lay on her dressing-table; the common familiar scent came to him. He thought: how generous she is, pretending that she's pleased I've come, but she can't be as stupid as that, she can't be as stupid as that.

He said: 'I got so wet,' but she interrupted him, 'Don't talk. Don't say anything. Come to bed,' and for a moment he was able to think: how foolish to imagine that home meant comfort, tenderness, knowledge, understanding; home is hunger about to be satisfied, bitterness about to be forgotten; that's all one wants of home. He said: 'I didn't mean to come. I couldn't keep away'; and saw her expression harden at the very moment when she took him in her arms. 'Don't talk,' Milly said. 'I hate you when you talk.'

5

'THERE'S been a man hanging about nearly all day,' Mrs Simpson said. She moved an ash-tray a few inches and flicked with a duster.

The Assistant Commissioner looked up sharply; he had known quite well that something worried her, for ever since he returned from the Yard she had been at him about one thing or another. Quite suddenly a few hours ago he had remembered that he was dining with Caroline Bury and had telephoned to say that he would not be at home for dinner and that his evening clothes must be laid out. Mrs Simpson liked a lot of warning; she was growing too old for her job, but the same would be said of him very soon and he had not the heart to dismiss her, not did he wish to go back to the silky domination of a manservant younger than himself.

'A man in dark striped trousers?' he asked.

'If I didn't think you'd be in any minute asking for something, ringing up,' Mrs Simpson added with unhappy scorn, 'I'd have gone out and given him a bit of my mind. He ought to have been ashamed of himself, wasting all the day like that. He was here at lunch time, he was here at tea time. While there are some people who have to work themselves to the bone.'

The Assistant Commissioner looked at his watch. 'I must be off in a few minutes.'

'You'll have a taxi?'

'No, no, I'll walk.'

'It would give me the creeps,' Mrs Simpson said, 'spending all the day with murderers and thieves. Why, I dream sometimes that you're bleeding on the doorstep.'

'Come, come, Mrs Simpson, this is London.'

'Them as knows what London is,' Mrs Simpson said, 'would not be surprised to find their nearest and dearest bleeding.'

'Well, I must be off. You mustn't have – er – these fancies.'

'Your tie needs straightening,' Mrs Simpson said. She turned her tongue against him as if it were a knife; in her harsh pulls at his black tie she seemed to put him in his place, to rebuke him for offering advice to someone older than himself, to someone who knew London so much better. She defended herself always in this way against the faintest hint of patronage. Ten years' seniority gave her the privilege of advising. 'You ought to take a taxi,' she said. 'I'd take a taxi,' but the advice from her was not convincing; it would have needed more than 'the creeps' to have broken the routine of a lifetime, the fitting on of the straw hat, the secure pinning of the brooch in the high-necked blouse, presently the slap, slap of old feet going down the street towards the Embankment, towards the trams.

'I must take exercise when I can get it, Mrs Simpson.'

'Get along with you. When you've reached your age you need a rest.' She flicked her way, apprehensively, to the window, ran the duster over the dustless gleaming pane, stared down into the dark street. 'I'll call a taxi.'

'No,' the Assistant Commissioner said and snapped his watch-case.

'I don't see why I should go home worrying, just because you won't take a taxi.' There was 'nothing to her' in her grey dress, her apron which had once been white; her grey hair was pulled tight on the top of her head into a bun no larger than an egg-cup. She was like a wisp of smoke at the window from an almost extinct fire. 'I've got enough to worry about.'

'Quite unnecessary,' the Assistant Commissioner said.

'I don't want to find a new job at my age.'

'But what was there about this man – ?'

'I didn't like his face.'

'You mustn't trust too much – '

Mrs Simpson laughed; it was, so far as he could remember, the first time he had heard her laugh. The laugh caught in the loose strings of her throat, and the sound was like a cough. 'You telling me,' she said. 'Faces. I can tell a face when I see one. Sixty years I've been in service. Nursery maid, nurse, cook, housekeeper. Why, I was even in the pantry once.' She had never been so self-revealing; the past she generally kept as securely concealed as her savings, which, he happened to know, lay flat, in india-rubber bands, at the bottom of a trunk. 'I didn't like his face,' she said, and her lips screwed up as if at the memory of innumerable faces which during sixty years of service she had disliked: the soft unformed faces of stupid children, employers who didn't know their own minds, vulgar women who railed because their food was a little burned. How she had suffered, she seemed to say, at vulgarity, obstinacy, stupidity; certainly, she didn't want another job at her age. 'I'm well suited here,' she strangely confessed.

'I promise you, Mrs Simpson, that I'll take a taxi if the man – er – becomes, becomes a nuisance.'

She had to be satisfied with that; one did not expect any generous response from an employer. 'The custard was a bit better today, Amy,' that was the kind of praise to which she was accustomed. Indeed any unreserved praise she had always met with suspicion as the prelude to some piece of cheeseparing, the demand for another dish from a joint already finished in the servants' hall.

'Well,' she said, 'you are old enough to take care of yourself, I suppose.' She surprised the Assistant Commissioner for the second time by fetching his coat and helping him into it; she had never done it before. She flicked at some dust on the hem with her cloth and left in its place several pieces of fluff which she had removed from under the sideboard. 'I suppose you'll be sitting up all night now. What you want to go out to dinner for with all those papers to read, I can't think.'

'It's an old friend.' She sniffed, following him down the stairs, and her little dark eyes were full of suspicion; she opened the front door and peered out before she let him by, kept her eyes on him as he stepped carefully over a sodden gutter, as he crossed the slippery shining rain-wet road to the opposite pavement. 'Anyway,' she screamed after him, 'you'll have to take a taxi home. There'll be more rain before night.'

Brown clouds blew up against all that was left of the moon; the air seemed to hold rain which had not yet begun to fall. One forced one's way as if through drenched washing hanging from a line. Nothing, the Assistant Commissioner thought, will induce me to take a taxi tonight; for they were skidding on the wet tarmac. The air was busy with the grinding of brakes, the shriek of sliding rubber, the heavy single drops of rain collecting on the leaves of plane trees and then sliding downwards to the pavements and the gravel walks. Everybody walked fast to get somewhere before the storm came, everybody but the Assistant Commissioner, whose liver felt the damp, whose head swam with the nausea of swamp and jungle and the hopeless East. Nobody played round the fountains; the water was tossed and tossed trivially between the darkened sky and the shaded pool.

Why is he following me? the Assistant Commissioner wondered apathetically; it's the same man. When he reached the pavement by the National Gallery, he looked back and saw at the far end of the Square the small black-clothed figure loitering by a lion. Between them were the electric standards and the smudged pavings and the rampart and nobody at all. He could come across and talk to me now. But the man only moved restlessly round the lion's base.

184

The Assistant Commissioner turned his back again and went on his way, up Charing Cross Road, down into the subway, up Tottenham Court Road, turned this way, turned that, conscious all the time of the figure very far behind. This can't go on indefinitely, he thought; he has the chance to speak to me tonight; tomorrow I shall be forced to have him detained and questioned. Then the eighteenth-century door, the sense of heavy curtains, crowded furniture, pictured walls, the expectation of someone who had died while he was abroad; and the thought of Justin spread a vacancy between chair and chair while he waited, until he felt himself a dried pea rattling in an empty pod.

That was what struck him too on seeing Caroline. It was not that she was ten years older; the years could make no impression on that haggard brightly painted face, whose beauty he could recognize more easily than other men because it had so often pitiably grimaced at him from the interior of eastern shrines; it was that she was not alive in the same way. She had lost her background; the slow and simple, the rubicund Justin was dead; her brilliance was no longer seen flashing against a rough brown tweeded curtain, it glowed, glittered, was lost in wide empty spaces of air. He wondered whether her charity, her passion to help, had been a little dulled, now that Justin was dead.

'How are you, Caroline?' She grimaced at him with a hand to her throat: 'The doctors say that I've got to go to the south. It's absurd, of course. Next week. . . .' So it had been true, he thought, after all. She trailed about in odd timeless garments; always she gave the impression of being dressed consciously for a monument in a manner which might not seem ridiculous when the fashions changed. 'Don't tell the others,' she croaked at him. 'Some of them are capable of following me.'

The Assistant Commissioner said with complete sincerity: 'You had always the, the power to inspire – er –

affection.' He was surprised when she laughed at him. 'Affection? Don't be absurd. They get what they can out of me. I'm a bit tired of them. I want to be alone.' But she was already alone; the Assistant Commissioner, the others (poets, painters, novelists and politicians) had no more ability to populate her brain than a set of ghosts; and the only ghost she would have welcomed did not appear: Justin, 'just up from the country', his thick platitudes threading the wit and the pretensions like the remnants of a sound old cloth in a much patched coat.

'I wanted you to come early,' Caroline Bury said, 'to ask you about Drover. People say he's going to be hanged. It's absurd.'

'Did you know him?' he asked her with surprise.

'I wish I had,' she said. 'I know them all too late.'

'Oh come, Caroline, you know – er – what is the phrase,' he brought it out with a touch of irony, 'everybody.'

'Too late,' she said. 'I know them when they've made a name.' She never troubled to explain herself; the bareness of her sentences contrasted with the intricacy of her handwriting; she offered innumerable opportunities to her enemies. Now it would have been possible for a malicious person to assume that she was complaining at not being able to discover and advertise talent. The Assistant Commissioner was not subtle; he found it easy to follow her; he knew that she regretted that her help was always given to those who were beginning to need no help. She said: 'You could help Drover.'

'It's out of my hands,' he said.

'Nonsense. Beale has asked you for a report.'

The Assistant Commissioner was startled. 'How do you know that?'

'His secretary told me.'

'That young man,' he said with distaste, 'is capable of doing, that's to say, he's – I don't like him.'

186

'What are you saying in your report?'

'Really, you know, Caroline, it's private.'

'Don't be absurd. You know you can trust me.'

But he could not trust her; it was impossible to trust anyone with so ardent, so unscrupulous a longing to help. Her charity had always been heroic; it had led her in and out of police courts; she had declaimed from innumerable witness-boxes; she had broken confidences, disclosed secrets, libelled and perjured in her desire to help.

'I came here to see you, Caroline, not to talk about Drover. The case is over; the appeal's been heard; you ought to talk – to talk to Beale.'

'He's a nonentity. I don't talk to nonentities.' Even the bric-à-brac supported her boast; the signed photograph of James, a great swollen brow floating over gloved hands; the cigarette box from the great dead Liberal leader; the pictures by Margaret Surrogate upon the wall.

'So Surrogate's gone Communist,' the Assistant Commissioner said, worming away from the subject of Drover.

'It's fashionable. But Margaret was a genius. Those pictures – '

He made a pretence of studying them. 'I'm afraid I don't understand pictures. Aren't they rather – artificial?'

Caroline Bury laughed with a hand on her thin throat. 'You and she are the most natural people I've ever known.'

The Assistant Commissioner was startled at the personality. He did not like to be connected with the woman who had painted those pictures; there was something about them hysterical and unhealthy; they smelt of sex as strongly as a bush of flowering May. 'I shall never like them.'

'Too phallic for you? Her husband, you see, didn't satisfy her.'

The Assistant Commissioner did not know where to look; his old yellow face set obstinately; he was familiar enough

187

with Caroline to recognize that her coarseness was calculated. She was angry with him and this was her way of
baiting him. 'Of course her dissatisfaction made her as an
artist. But what happens to the wives of all the men you shut
up? They take in washing, don't they? They don't paint. I
suppose they all find a man somewhere.'

'You've got a low view, Caroline, of human nature.'

'Here I am trying to do something for Drover, and all the
time I'm forgetting Drover's wife. He's got one, hasn't he?
What will she do if he's reprieved? Oughtn't I to be urging
you to see that he's hanged?'

'This is all Beale's business.'

'Don't be absurd. He's waiting for your advice.'

'Well, if you must know, Caroline, I'll tell you. I'm simply
writing that it will have no effect, whether he hangs Drover
or reprieves him. Beale always imagines the country's on the
edge of revolution. The truth is, nobody cares about anything but his own troubles. Everybody's too busy fighting
his own little battle to think of the, the next man. Except
you, Caroline.' He had never said so much to her at one
time.

'Dinner is served.'

'Are we alone, Caroline?' he asked with astonishment.

'Yes,' she croaked at him, 'alone,' and trailed before him
to the door in her absurd, her expensive, her timeless dress.
She might have added that they were alone, so far as she
knew, in not caring for their own troubles, for not fighting
their own battle in ignorance of the general war.

'Really,' the Assistant Commissioner said, sitting down
opposite her. He stopped and cleared his throat; he had forgotten the bowed head and the mumbled grace; impossible
to catch the words, which were neither English nor Latin.
'Really,' he began again as the gaunt unhappy face lifted.
'I'm, you know, honoured.'

'You are busy and I'm tired. If you won't help me over

Drover, there's no more to be said.' But the Assistant Commissioner doubted that. 'I wanted to see you anyway before this absurd operation.'

'Operation? You never told me there was to be an operation?'

'You would think me quite capable of inventing it to get what I wanted.'

'You are certainly the most – er – generous.' He found himself to his own amazement absurdly moved by the sharp cynical features opposite him. 'The most noble.' He hummed and ha-ed for want of words; suddenly, dangerously, he wanted to offer her anything she asked of him. She had never, he believed, received anything from anyone except Justin; she had given and given, time and money and nerves. 'You are very brave,' he concluded.

'No,' she said, 'I'm frightened of pain. I've never been able to stand pain. That's why I'm cross and worried and unwilling to see people. I've been trying to make a will. But there's no individual I want to leave money to, and I won't leave it to the State as it's run at present; it would help to buy a few aeroplanes or tanks.'

'The hospitals?'

'It's banal, but I suppose I shall have to. Now I should have liked to help Drover, but Beale would be frightened of taking a bribe, I suppose?' It was another of her fantastic tactless plans.

'Caroline, Caroline, we aren't in South America.'

'I've been told that before, but I'm not convinced. Do you believe in the way the country is organized? Do you believe that wages should run from thirty shillings a week to fifteen thousand a year, that a manual labourer should be paid less than a man who works with his brains? They are both indispensable, they both work the same hours, they are both dog-tired at the end of their day. Do you think I've the right to leave two hundred thousand pounds to anyone I like?'

189

'No.'

'But you support it. You support it more than any other single man. Without the police force such a state of affairs couldn't last a year.'

'Who would take the place of Beale and – er – the others? Surrogate?'

'He's absurd, of course, but it's not a difficult thing to run a department of state. It's not so difficult as running a farm or driving an engine. There's a lot of pretence about these things. Put one of Beale's clerks in Beale's place, and he'd do as well as Beale.'

'It hasn't been tried. It's too dangerous.'

'It has been tried.'

'Russia,' the Assistant Commissioner said with distress; 'we don't want starvation here.'

'We've got starvation here. It's only that you and I don't share it.'

The Assistant Commissioner fell silent; automatically his fork dipped and dipped; he had no idea what he was eating. Caroline Bury said: 'It would be maddening to die now, with the world in the state it is, if one hadn't Faith.'

'Faith?'

'Faith.'

'Christianity, you mean?'

'No, no, not Christianity.' He waited with his fork poised and wondered whether the problem of Caroline Bury's religion was to be solved at last; from the drawing-room came a faint smell of incense cones slowly burning. 'You mean – just faith,' he prompted her.

'Well, haven't you faith?'

'Well,' he said, 'of course one – er – hopes,' and crumbled his bread and found himself again faced with the question; how can so cynical, so clear-sighted a woman bemuse herself with incense, Indian idols (there were several in the spare

190

bedrooms), ikons (there was one on the staircase), pictures of the Virgin (they were everywhere)?

'What do you hope?'

'Well,' he said, 'one lives and then, that is, one dies.' It was the nearest he could come to conveying his sense of a great waste, a useless expenditure of lives: Caroline in the operating theatre, Drover on the scaffold, the girl on Streatham Common, Justin in Spain. It was impossible to believe in a great directing purpose, for these were not spare parts which could be matched again. He was filled, under the shadow of retirement, beneath the nausea which fogged his sight as he rose too quickly from the table, with a passionate desire for an eternal life, but an eternal life on earth watching the world grow reasonable, watching nationalities die and economic chaos giving way to order. But when that time came, he thought, it would not be enjoyed by the most selfless: Justin was dead; Caroline would be dead, several men in his old company whom he had admired. . . . It would be enjoyed arbitrarily by certain people who happened to be alive in a certain century, by adventurers and politicians and swindlers among the rest. Those who had fought hardest for it would probably be dead. That he himself would be dead was not unfair; he had not helped; he had served those who paid him; he had stood aside. But Caroline who had wanted to bribe the Home Secretary with an inheritance deserved to live, and following her trailing dress back to the incense and the shaded crowded room he felt small and mean and ashamed. His excuse had always been that he did his job, but remembering Justin he thought: she did her job, but she did a great deal more.

'I must be going,' he said.

'And you can't help with Drover?'

'I'm sorry, Caroline.'

'Good night then.' She held out a bony chalk-white hand. 'You used to find your own way out.'

'Yes, yes,' he said and realized suddenly how old they were, two old people who could not part with any warmth but who should have been able to part with greater ease. 'I'm sorry,' he said again and thought: it's lucky she has got Faith, whatever she means by it, she's got nothing else: an ageing haggard woman in a dark room crowded with the relics of a taste which had been enthusiastic, never impeccable.

He searched a long while in the unlit hall for the Yale latch. She was an unconventional woman; she did not care for a maid to shut the door behind a friend as if he were a stranger; she wanted to give the impression of a door always open. But it would be more convenient in that case if the light were left turned on. He pulled himself up; he had nearly joined all her other friends in criticizing her. His hand found the latch, pushed the door open; he had forgotten while he had been with her the man who so persistently followed him. At the top of the three worn steps he remembered. The man stood in the middle of the street and held something forward in his hand. For a moment the Assistant Commissioner failed to recognize what it was.

When he saw that it was a revolver, he quietly closed the door of number fifteen. He did not want Caroline startled if anything happened. He was not afraid; he was supremely confident; his spirits rose like a rocket through the mist of indecision, dissatisfaction, regret; they dropped his ageing body to earth like the rocket's stick, while they soared higher. But though his spirits soared, he was not reckless; he knew exactly what he had to do. He must remain still, make no sudden movement; with any luck at all a taxi would presently appear, or a car might be driven between them and give him an opportunity to cross the pavement. He held the man's gaze, standing there three steps above him –

*

as yellow as the light behind the shoulder, old, calm, the enemy, the joker outside the Berkeley. 'A pram on a taxi,' and the fume of hatred smouldering at the base of the brain rose and coiled and rose, and the fingers tightened and one thought: Now. Shall I fire now? Where must I aim? At the top stud of his evening shirt? But my hand is shaking. I must be calm. If he moves an inch I'll fire; but old, calm, yellow in the face, with his thin lips and his upper class lids, he waited, and one thought: He knows I'll miss. Have I come all this way, tracked him down so many pavements, waited and waited without food, only to miss him in the end because my hand shakes? And one thought again: If a car comes I must fire at once. I mustn't wait. There's nobody in the world who wouldn't help him against me. I'm alone.

He was separated from everyone he loved by his hatred. But when the shot was fired and the man was dead, his hatred would leave him. He would have let it run its course and it would leave him. And he thought of the dark steep stairs he had trodden at prostitutes' heels and afterwards was calm again, except for the dim feeling that this was not the kind of life a man should have to lead. His hand rose, he did not look at the other's face but at the top stud in his evening shirt, somewhere a car hooted, he was aware, at the edge of the left eye, of headlamps blasting the darkness at the top of the long Bloomsbury street . . .

Then, I said to Milly, I fired. You told me that I could never hold a gun, but my hand was still for long enough. He fell down the three steps and lay in the road. The car tried to stop, but the road was slippery after the rain, and it skidded fifty feet. I put the pistol in my pocket and came away. I hated you last night, but now I hate no one. I feel quite at ease again. They will not trace me, because he does not know me, and I had so little motive for anger against him. I love you now without hatred or jealousy or lust. It is as if I had driven my own nightmare into his body through the hole the bullet made.

He was telling himself a fairy tale; but this was true: his hate narrowed to a stud in a man's shirt, the headlights of a great car splashing the road and pavement between them, the thought: he'll run when it comes between. He steadied his hand; somebody shouted to him and he heard the brakes grind and the wheels scream as they failed to hold the surface of the road; he took his final aim at the man outside the door, at the policeman in the witness-box, at the jester outside the Berkeley, at the director's nephew, at the manager, at the voices calling, 'Conrad, Conrad', across the asphalt yard. You can't frighten me with the name of murderer: Jim is a murderer. He pulled and pulled and the rusty trigger did not move. Then he was struck in the body and thrown a dozen yards and could not think: what has done this? nor wonder: why am I here? lying with his face over the pavement edge, watching the black water trickle down the gutter and fall through a grating, aware of pain and voices and pain, pain in the back and a worse pain in the jaw (the dentist's drill ground and ground and Milly came up the church and the smell of anthracite choked him).

'Do you know him, sir?'

'I haven't any idea who he is.'

'The ambulance is coming.'

'He wouldn't have done any damage; the revolver's loaded with blanks.'

Mr Bernay said: 'You'll have to pay me for the risk,' and smiled and checked the smile and blew his nose. He thought: soon I shall be unconscious, nobody could bear this pain for long, and as the great drill thrust again between his teeth, he tried to move, he tried to scream, but he could hear nothing but the voices talking: 'Really, you know it wasn't our fault. He stepped forward. The road's so slippery.' Again he tried to scream, because pain was scratching now like little sharp

194

finger-nails at his spine, and this time he heard: the sound was a low grunt. It gave no satisfaction. Pain was like a bird frantic for freedom, dashing from wall to wall of the imprisoning room; his brain was bruised with the beat of its wings. Again and again he flung the window wide as it drove towards the glass, but back it went to the furthest wall: beaten and bruised and never exhausted. If I could faint, he thought, if I could scream.

'Better not move him; his back may be broken.' His hand touched the black water trickling in the gutter; he could see his own blood joining the water, flowing thickly off the pavement edge. The bird ceased to blunder back and forth in his brain; it was resigned; it lay in a corner exhausted; it knew that it could never get out. The words which people spoke dropped slowly through the air: 'Listen . . . I . . . can . . . hear . . . it . . . coming.' He could hear each word drop from the lips and his brain shrank with fear, waiting for the sound to reach him and pierce him like an aerial dart on the base of the skull. Even light was retarded; the headlights brushed the street slowly like a yellow broom. Somebody knelt on the pavement beside him, and the slight touch of the overcoat on Conrad's side stung like iodine on an open sore.

But when they lifted him the bird was roused again; the walls of the brain throbbed and trembled with its assaults; if I could scream, if I could faint.

He remained conscious and they lifted him into an ambulance and a police constable and an attendant sat beside him and they drove back the way he had walked. He could tell when they reached Trafalgar Square, because they drove round and round for what seemed a long while in a circle. Then he was out in the street, he was carried up steps and he tried to scream, and Big Ben struck the half-hour. He was on a wheeled bed passing down long corridors, nurses walked the opposite way and stared at him and he tried to scream;

he was in a small room and they held a little box in front of his face and he tried to scream. Then the pain became unbearable and he closed his eyes and opened them and Milly sat beside him and a metal flask hung above his head and a tube dropped saliva into his mouth and he felt no pain. The pain, he knew, was still there, but it was exhausted, it lay still and cramped in a corner, stiff with the bandages which confined him too; one pretended not to notice it; everyone walked softly on tiptoe not to wake it.

They had put screens round his bed, but through a gap he could see the wards, rows of men wearily sleeping, and a sister sitting reading at a table where one light burned. Milly bent forward over the bed. 'They found a note for me in your pocket.' He tried to answer her, but he could not move his bandaged jaw; the artificial saliva dripped, dripped on his tongue.

'What was the use, Conrad, what was the use?'

He could not answer her. He tried to convey through his eyes some hint of the pain it caused him to be questioned and to be unable to reply.

'Why didn't you ask me first, Conrad?' She leant her face close to his and whispered: 'What was the good? Why couldn't you have waited?' He stared back at the skin drawn tightly over the bone and tried to raise his hand. But he was strapped and plastered and he could not move.

'You couldn't have thought it would do any good?' He struggled to answer her. The nurse came round the screen and whispered: 'You mustn't talk to him. You'd better go.'

Milly put her hands on the edge of the bed and whispered with desperation, 'I must tell him – I've got to tell him – about Jim,' but the nurse pulled at her arm and said: 'Tomorrow. You'll excite him. He's got to be quiet.' She looked down at him; he could tell at once how bad was the news she had received; and he struggled to understand. It was as if all the impressions of the room, the sight which had been wasted on the screen, on the nurse, on the ranged beds, could be driven back into his brain to reinforce the vitality he needed if he was to understand: he closed his eyes. He closed his ears to every trivial sound, the pinned watch ticking over the nurse's heart, the breathing of men asleep, the drip of saliva down the rubber tube, so that he might only hear what the nurse and Milly whispered. He pushed his toes against the bed's end, feeling the iron cold through sheet and blankets, drawing all his remaining strength to one centre, so that before she went he would have power, in spite of bandages and plaster, to sit upright, to move his jaw and speak, asking her what it was she had heard of Jim.

He opened his eyes and saw Milly, quite clearly, in relief against the reading-lamp, blackness all round her, and he was aware that she was bewildered and hopeless and needed him and that he was dying; it seemed to him that she was watching him with horror as if he was the first of all the men whom sooner or later she must come to know; he unsealed his ears and heard the breathing catch in her throat. He put his foot against the rail and urged his jaw to open, his muscles to respond; then there was pain and a sense of something breaking and the taste of blood and his throat filling and a struggle to breathe.

He never knew that he screamed in spite of his broken jaw; but with curious irrelevance, out of the darkness, after they had left him and his pulses had ceased beating and he was dead, consciousness returned for the fraction of a second, as if his brain had been a hopelessly shattered mirror, of which one piece caught a passing light. He saw and his brain recorded the sight: twelve men lying uneasily awake in the public ward with wireless headpieces clamped across their ears, and a nurse reading under a lamp, and nobody beside his bed.

*

197

Incomprehensible, the Assistant Commissioner thought, incomprehensible. He trod slowly up the stairs step by step, paused at the landing: a steel engraving of Frith's 'Railway Station' (the thief in handcuffs, the abandoned wife), on an occasional table a naked bronze child withdrawing a thorn from his foot. He opened the door of his flat, and the light gleamed on the carved gourds and flashed back from the native spears. A middle-aged man rose from the one armchair. 'Your housekeeper let me in.' He hesitated. 'You don't remember me.'

'I remember you, of course,' the Assistant Commissioner said. 'You used to be chaplain at Leeds Prison. You've been – er – transferred here.'

'I wanted to see you.' He hesitated: a pale man in a heavy tweed suit with an ordinary collar and tie.

'Give me one moment,' the Assistant Commissioner said. 'I've just been shot at – with a blank cartridge.' It was the blank cartridge which worried him. He went into his bedroom and sponged his face. 'Forgive my keeping you waiting,' he called through the door. But the chaplain was glad of the delay; he never found it easy to speak directly. Since he entered the prison service fifteen years before, his life had been spent in breaking things gently, the deaths of relatives, the treachery of wives. It had affected his manner, so that now he could not speak directly on any subject; he broke his views on wine, the theatre, revised prayer books, with interminable circumlocutions. The Assistant Commissioner watched him in the mirror of the dressing table, as he stood uneasily in front of a skin shield and tried to find words.

'You know Beale's secretary?'

They progressed very slowly towards understanding: one, old and inarticulate and thinking all the time of the blank cartridge; the other middle-aged and shy, and, as it soon appeared, angry and unhappy.

'That young man been talking again?'

'He told me you were advising the Minister about Drover.'

'He seems to have told everyone. I am – er – prejudiced against that young man.' He squeezed out his sponge. 'Won't you sit down?' But in the mirror he could see that the chaplain preferred to roam; he took up a gourd and examined it, touched the edge of a spear.

'I'm going to resign.'

The Assistant Commissioner examined his hands; on one cuff there was a smear of blood. 'Will you excuse me while I, that is, change my shirt?' He picked out the links slowly: a blank cartridge; never seen him before; incomprehensible.

'I'm going to resign,' the chaplain repeated.

'I'm sorry,' the Assistant Commissioner said. 'I've heard often – how much the men like you.'

The chaplain said: 'I can't stand human justice any longer. Its arbitrariness. Its incomprehensibility.'

'I don't mean, of course, to be, to be blasphemous, but isn't that very like, that is to say, isn't divine justice much the same?'

'Perhaps. But one can't hand in a resignation to God.'

The Assistant Commissioner took off his shirt and searched in a drawer. Through the open door he could see the chaplain fidgeting with a wooden tobacco jar.

'And I have no complaint against His mercy.' He was coming to the end of the long and rambling road; the object of his visit was in sight. He said with sudden fury: 'Of course I am a fool to be here. Red-tape. Bureaucracy. Once a thing is done, it can't be undone.' The Assistant Commissioner put in his links. 'It's quite useless, I suppose, to ask you to undo the mischief when once you've done it?'

'Really,' the Assistant Commissioner said, 'I don't, don't understand – '

'They've acted on your advice.'

The Assistant Commissioner tied his tie. 'You mean the execution – '

'It's off. They've reprieved him.'

The Assistant Commissioner came back into his sitting-room and sat down. 'I haven't sent them my report. I haven't even written it. I think they ought to have let me know. It would have saved me a good deal of time, of trouble. As you see, I've got, got a lot of work to do.'

'The Governor had a message from the Home Office this evening. As usual, of course, it was I who had to break the news.'

'The good news.'

The chaplain said: 'I had no illusions about that. Drover wasn't afraid of death, but he's very fond of his wife. She'll be a middle-aged woman when he comes out of prison; do you think any woman can be faithful for eighteen years to a man she sees once a month? And they love each other.'

'What did he say?'

'He said nothing. He's not a talkative man. But when they were taking him to one of the top cells in Block A, he tried to kill himself. He flung himself over. Of course he was only bruised. The wire net caught him. Have you got a drink?'

The Assistant Commissioner opened a cupboard. 'I'm sorry, the bottle's empty.'

'Never mind. I'm glad you weren't mixed up in this. There's only one comfort: he's got a brother. They're devoted to each other. He'll look after the wife. Well,' he looked helplessly round him, 'if you haven't sent in your report, I suppose there's nothing you can do. The man must live.' He said with an irony which was quite lost on the Assistant Commissioner: 'Beale has decided.'

'He should have decided in the first place,' the Assistant Commissioner said. 'He had the judge's notes.' The chaplain found his hat. He did nothing so definite as to shake hands, a man prematurely old, a man bent under the misery of many deaths, he wavered at the door. 'Eighteen years,' he said, almost dumb with the misery of too protracted a life.

'I shouldn't resign,' the Assistant Commissioner said, 'if I were you,' but his advice was rejected with less circumlocution than the chaplain had shown for a long while: 'It's already in writing'; and after he had gone and the telephone bell had checked the Assistant Commissioner's hand on the first leaf of the latest report, he found himself doubting his own statement. 'If I were you,' he had said. Now the voice from the hospital was telling him: 'He's dead. We've got his name. It's Conrad Drover. He's the brother of . . .'; and the Commissioner thought: Resign? He's right. I'm half inclined to resign myself.

The voice vibrated over the wire: the threatened storm was breaking: hummed and whistled through the black orifice. 'The operation was successful. Death due to shock. The only thing we can't find out is why he loaded with blank . . .' The voice faded; it could hardly be distinguished as it promised a full report, wished the Assistant Commissioner good night; and the first spatter of rain brushed the panes, blew through an open window, damped the papers on the desk.

Resign? He rose, shut the window, drew the curtains. The word seemed to usher him into an empty room, cold, fireless, without light, a room in which he might have expected company, but the only sign of their former presence was in the litter they had left behind them: the cigarette ash, the empty coffee-cups, which showed they had once been there, but had gone on.

He sat down again at his desk. I am a coward, he told himself; I haven't the courage of my convictions; I am not indispensable to the Yard; it is the Yard which is indispensable to me. He began to read the papers before him, but it was not his conscious mind which took their meaning in. If I had faith, he thought wryly; if I had any conviction that

I was on the right side; Caroline has that; when she loses it, she has only to change her side.

Then without warning, from his dissatisfaction and self-distrust and shame, his spirits rose; all that worried him dropped away, like the little figures running back from the landing ground as an airship lifts. He was alone in the wide phosphorescent air with his idea. He forgot the chaplain, he forgot Drover, he forgot the blank cartridge. He began to write in his small meticulous handwriting across the top of the Streatham report: 'What the officers in charge of this case have not realized is the significance of the prostitute's evidence that she saw Flossie Matthews waiting on a Park chair as early as 6 p.m. Taken in conjunction with the other evidence. . . .' It was for these moments of unsought revelation that the Assistant Commissioner lived.

Graham Greene

Our Man in Havana

Agent 59200/5 Wormold invented the stories he sent to the British Secret Service from Cuba . . . and the results surprised him most of all.

Travels With My Aunt

Henry Pulling retired from the bank to grow dahlias. But he hadn't reckoned with his Aunt Augusta, who snatched him out of suburban Southwood, to join her on a madcap trip to Brighton, Paris, Istanbul, Paraguay . . .

The End of the Affair

This frank, intense account of a love-affair and its mystical aftermath takes place in a suburb of war-time London.

A Burnt-out Case

Philip Toynbee described this novel, set in a leper colony in the Congo, as being 'perhaps the best that he has ever written'.

Graham Greene

Brighton Rock

Set in the pre-war Brighton underworld, this is the story of a teenage gangster, Pinkie, and Ida, his personal Fury, who relentlessly brings him to justice.

The Power and the Glory

This poignant story set during an anti-clerical purge in one of the southern states of Mexico 'starts in the reader an irresistible emotion of pity and love' – *The Times*

The Comedians

In this novel, Graham Greene makes a graphic study of the committed and the uncommitted in the present-day tyranny of Haiti.

The Quiet American

This novel makes a wry comment on European interference in Asia in its story of the Franco-Vietminh war in Vietnam.

The Heart of the Matter

Scobie – a police officer in a West African colony – was a good man, but his struggle to maintain the happiness of two women destroyed him.

V. S. Naipaul

'It is time . . . for him to be quite simply recognised as this country's most talented and promising young writer' – Antony Powell in the *Daily Telegraph*

The Mimic Men

Living in a run-down London suburb, Ralph Singh, a disgraced colonial minister exiled from the Caribbean island of his birth, is writing his biography. When he comes to politics he finds himself caught up in the upheaval of empire, in the turmoil of too-large events which move too fast . . .

A House for Mr Biswas

Mohun Biswas wants success, a house and a portion of land of his own. As he moves from job to job, acquiring a wife and four children, the odds against him lengthen and his ambition becomes more remote.

The Mystic Masseur

Ganesh, who cured the Woman Who Couldn't Eat and the Man Who Made Love to His Bicycle, becomes involved in a local scandal. But he manages to keep some surprises in reserve . . .

Also published:

Miguel Street

In a Free State

The Suffrage of Elvira

Mr Stone and the Knights Companion

Lionel Davidson

The Night of Wenceslas

'Invited' to Prague on what seems to be an innocent business trip, Young Nicholas Whistler finds himself trapped – between the Cold War and the hot clutches of the amorous and statuesque Vlasta.

The Rose of Tibet

Charles Houston should never have been in Tibet in the first place; he only went there to find his missing brother. But the Chinese invade, and he must get out fast – with Chinese soldiers and the cruel Himalayan winter right behind him.

Making Good Again

Lionel Davidson plunges into the aftermath of the Second World War. A claim for reparations sends James Raison into a whirlpool of conflicting identity and age-old hate.

The Sun Chemist

As the oil crisis overturns the economies of the West, Igor Druyanov is on the trail of the philosopher's stone, a formula for synthetic oil left by the great Chaim Weizmann on his death-bed. And the political consequences of such a formula, as the reader will understand, are enormous . . .